EAST OF A

Russell Atwood

BALLANTINE BOOKS

NEW YORK

A Ballantine Book
Published by The Ballantine Publishing Group

Copyright © 1999 by Russell Atwood

Map by Mapping Specialists, Ltd.

Grateful acknowledgment is made to Harvard University Press for permission to reprint an excerpt from Poem # 135 from *The Poems of Emily Dickinson*, Thomas H. Johnson, ed., Cambridge, Mass., The Belknap Press of Harvard University Press. Copyright © 1951, 1955, 1979, 1983 by the President and Fellows of Harvard College. Reprinted by permission of the publishers and the Trustees of Amherst College.

www.randomhouse.com/BB/

Library of Congress Cataloging-in-Publication Data
Atwood, Russell.
East of A / Russell Atwood.— 1st ed.
p. cm.
ISBN 0-345-42776-9 (alk. paper)
I. Title.
PS3551. T87E28   1998
813' .54—dc21   98-19610

Manufactured in the United States of America

First Edition: February 1999

10   9   8   7   6   5   4   3   2   1

THIS BOOK IS DEDICATED TO MY PARENTS,
RUSS AND MARY ATWOOD, WHO ALWAYS
ENCOURAGED MY INVESTIGATIONS.

ACKNOWLEDGMENTS

Supreme thanks to my unlicensed writing coach, Walt Taylor, who, as usual, did everything but get paid; my faithful editors, Joe Blades (Ballantine) and Janet Hutchings *(EQMM)*; the bosses who cut me loose at the right time, Terry Byrne and Anne Reischick; and my tireless team of irregulars who keep me from writing absolute fiction: Dori Poole, Jerry Schwartz, Mollena Williams, Jenny Rosenstrach, Ellie Fitzgerald, Bennett Coleman, Kim Fritschy, Jean-Marie Atwood, Patricia Guy, Charles Wright, Laura Cruger Fox, Nina Nusynowitz, John Patterson (and everyone at Porto Rico), Amanda Stern, Martha Friedlander, Rick Shrout, Julian Nobrega, and Karen Clark Smith.

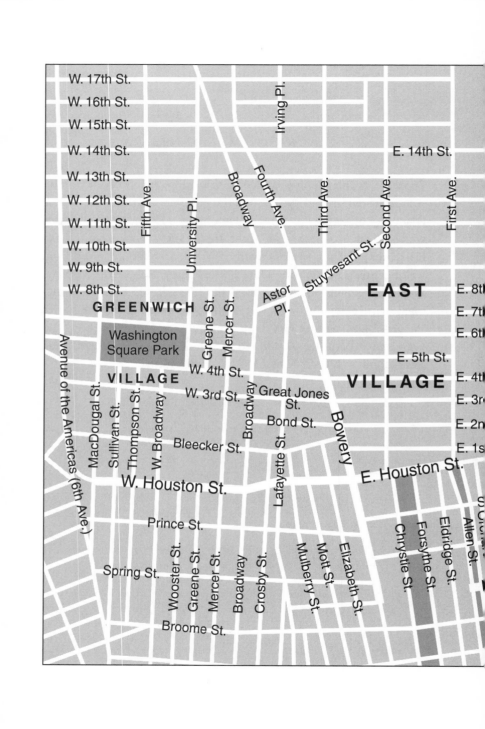

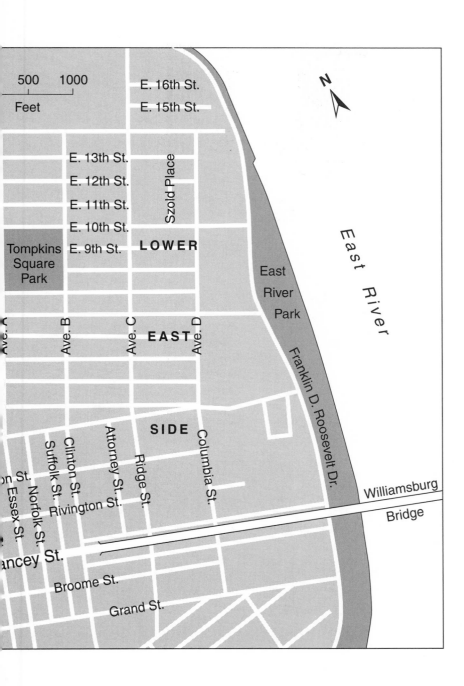

EAST OF A

I'd been out of town, upstate in Syracuse, nine days snatching whatever sun and country atmosphere I could between court appearances in a child-custody case, presenting surveillance evidence against the natural mother. After the case finally settled late Thursday afternoon, I dropped off the rental and caught an evening bus back to the city. Slept most of the way, dozing off listening to a tape of Joe Mantegna reading *Farewell, My Lovely* till the batteries ran down:

"I was a swell guy. I en-joyyed . . . be-inng . . . mmmmmm—"

The Peter Pan bus downshifted and swerved, slowing to approach the Lincoln Tunnel. Out my darkly tinted window, the etched-black skyline of Manhattan stood imposing and beautiful against a moonless May night. At first glimpse, my heart surged (almost alive again, not quite) like the last time I saw her—Clair, my sweet Air—fresh and lovely as I always remembered.

From that distance, the city stays the city of your imagination: a scintillating island of promises, of hope, of love renewed. Not until you get closer is the sobering truth revealed: you're happier to see her than she is you. Not angry, not resentful. Worse. Uninterested, dispassionate, preoccupied; her reticence inspires myth.

But eventually you get over it, they say, because reality (whatever that happens to be) sets in, and you take her for what she is: not *yours*—never your city—but just a city of her own.

I got into my office/apartment overlooking Twelfth Street and Second Avenue at half-past one in the morning with a week's worth of mail in my hand. While I was gone, no one had broken in. I counted the answering machine's flashes—nine—and decided I needed to eat something first, which meant going right back out again. The fridge naturally was empty, nothing but a single ice cube in the ice tray and an open box of baking soda.

I was overdressed for the East Village after midnight, still in my dark blue suit, narrow maroon tie, and shiny black shoes from my final court appearance. But I didn't change into street clothes because I was only going down to the Chungs' all-night deli, and I thought they'd get a kick out of seeing me looking so respectable. I was going to kid Mrs. Chung that the outfit was one of my disguises. Then she'd rattle off some English I couldn't follow one word of, but I'd laugh when she laughed.

Except when I got to the deli, the rusted accordian gates barred the doors and a big FOR RENT sign hung behind the plate glass in the darkened window. I peered in. The aisles and shelves were bare. One solitary fluorescent light fixture blinked on and off, spasmodically.

Couldn't digest it at first—I'd only been gone *nine days*. I still owed them for a pack of cigarettes. Why would they . . . ?

I'd have to ask around in the morning. The more immediate

problem was, where to shop now? Less than a block away, another convenience store on Second, but they overcharged (probably why they were still in business), so instead I turned west on East Twelfth, toward an indelectable deli on Third Avenue. The cashier who rang up my cigarettes, gallon of milk, and box of Cheerios wasn't the least bit impressed by my suit.

Rather than walk back the way I'd come, I went home on Eleventh. For no other reason, I suppose, than that I have an inclination to complete circles.

At the Third Avenue corner was the wide stone-block entrance to an NYU dorm, lit up stark orange by sodium-vapor floodlamps. Farther down Eleventh, the sidewalks narrowed and the lighting grew softer. Every five feet a thin, budding tree cast a spidery shadow—like cataracts—across a brick-face wall, the walls mostly belonging to prewar townhouses undergoing reconstruction. No lights on in any windows.

It was a minor through street, at that hour no traffic at all. Quaint and peaceful.

For a moment I even forgot where I was, imagining myself back in Syracuse, strolling down a country lane. The impression was furthered by the last stretch of block, taken up by St. Mark's-in-the-Bowery, a late Georgian church of rough-hewn stone and brick, and its adjoining churchyard housing the burial vaults of some of colonial New York's founding families, all surrounded by a spiked, Italianate cast-iron fence. I looked up; the high steeple clock read a quarter to two. Out of habit, I checked it against my wristwatch. And as quickly, let my coat sleeve drop back down.

I still had on my gold Rolex. My $3,500, perpetual-motion, date-day-chronometer, *gold* Rolex. I'd been out of the city too long. The watch was the most expensive piece—the only piece—of jewelry that I owned. Upstate, I'd worn it every day, walking through town without inhibition, my shirtsleeves rolled up, the Rolex glinting in the sun.

Something was wrong with my sleeve. I looked down; my coat

cuff was snagged on the watchband's crown clasp. I wanted to fix it, but first had to switch hands carrying the cereal and jug of milk; before I could, I heard a zipper zip up ahead.

From behind a scaly elm tree, eight feet away, a lean figure in black leather jacket and baggy camouflage fatigues stepped out and onto the sidewalk, briefly glanced my way, turned, and started walking in the other direction.

Some guy pissing against a car, I thought, and thought nothing of it, just continued walking. Strolling really, at the leisured pace I'd adopted while away. Nothing close to my usual urban-locomotion. Even so, I began to shorten the gap separating us, catching up without trying and certainly without wanting to.

I got a sudden uncomfortable feeling that the sharp slap of my footsteps was being listened to, concentrated on, measured.

Welcome home, Payton.

But I kept walking—had to—I couldn't cross the street just there because the cars parked at the curb were packed too closely. And I couldn't stop suddenly because it might've set him off. And I couldn't run the other way either, because . . . well, this was where I lived and worked, and I had to be able to walk around my own block. Right?

So, I kept walking. Walking. And getting closer. Closer.

I couldn't tell how either—whether he was taking baby steps or moonwalking—and as I approached, I wasn't even so sure it was a guy anymore. The black hair, cut in a spiky, androgynous crew, came to a lean point on the nape of the neck, pointing to a tattoo of a flaming blue star in a jagged blue circle. Silver rings in both small pinched ears—but what did that mean nowadays? Height: five-five. Build: concealed by the baggy clothes. Hands: out of view, held in front. Holding what?

Blind larvae hatched in my belly.

As my footsteps got closer, the head didn't stir an inch—weird in itself. The neck muscles just tensed and the skin on either side stood like dorsal fins.

I had to pass on either the right or the left. I chose the right; in a pinch, I could've dived over the hood of a parked car.

As we came side by side, I kept my eyes straight ahead on Second Avenue half a block away: cabs, buses, a darkened Mister Softee truck rolling by still playing its happy jingle. At the corner was a lighted pay phone, the receiver off the hook, swaying by its silver cord.

I was keyed up to spring at the slightest movement or sound. From the corner of my eye, I saw a pale face: dark eyebrows, low cheekbones, snub nose, and a cleft chin like flexed knuckles. I heard the high, uneven whistle of nose-breathing, and smelled a heavy, dusky sweetness: patchouli oil, stifling and repellent.

Then I was out in front, upwind, walking away, my back wide open to attack.

Now my ears were the ones carefully listening to footsteps behind, this time the slow clomp of loose-laced boots, trying to calculate their distance . . . gauge their intent.

And nothing happened.

Maybe after all it was just an ordinary case of pedestrian leapfrog, that nervous game we New Yorkers play daily—the ones who leave their apartments. But just in case I was wrong, I continued to listen, to focus my attention behind me. All of it.

Which is how I missed *them*—crouched low in the recessed entryway of a semibasement—until I was right alongside, and one softly snorted.

I flinched but kept facing forward, my vision going wide to horse-glimpse.

There were three of them, three stooges—all Curly—bald-headed behemoths with bull necks and beefy arms dressed in flak jackets and blue jeans.

Every advantage in the world—theirs—to have grabbed me as I went by, dragged me down, and gone to work on me in peace.

But they didn't. They weren't interested in me. I walked on by, took three more steps, and didn't turn when I heard a shrill yelp, followed by the scuffle of boots, and then—silence. Relative silence: car horns blaring in the distance, a flatbed truck clobbering a pothole, somewhere, some man's faint angry rant against the government going ignored. When I came to a street-level doorway, I turned and stepped in.

Peeking from the doorway, I saw only empty sidewalk and a head poking out from a stairwell. One of the Curlys acting as lookout, anxiously stealing glances back and descending another step for a better look at what was going on below.

I was curious, too.

Twenty feet to my left, the hustle and not so much the bustle of Second Avenue. Only seconds to reach the pay phone there and dial the local precinct (always quicker than 911). But response time being what it is—anywhere from five to thirty minutes—the whole thing might've been over and everyone on their way before a unit was even dispatched.

But so what? For all I knew they had a legitimate beef—just cause—for ganging up three against one. I couldn't imagine what that could be, but that still didn't make it any of my business. Between instinct and action, always a membrane of reason.

The lookout's head pricked up, as if he'd been summoned, and he left his post, going below to join the others.

So I stepped from the doorway and started back, walking on the balls of my feet over to the four steep, crumbling concrete steps leading down to the half basement, a dusty patio eight feet wide extending to a boarded-up door under a black iron staircase.

There, in the shadows, the four of them crowded.

I ducked down behind a row of lidded garbage cans and watched. I could see now it was definitely a woman, nearly a girl, her face like a tough little boy's. Wide dark eyes, a small blunt nose, and full lips sputtering to speak—but one of the men savagely cut her off.

"No, you listen! LSD wants back his—"

"But I didn't—!"

He snatched her throat and pinched it shut with hairy sausage fingers, each ringed by silver bands.

The other two men grabbed the girl's arms and legs as she started to kick, her face suffusing lavender, eyeballs distending hard-boiled.

I stood up. I was still clutching my groceries. I put down the bag with the cereal, but liked the reassuring weight of the gallon jug of milk in my fist. I switched my grip on it, pointing the spout down, and hefted it a couple times like a cudgel. Better than nothing. I began.

"Goddamn," the man was growling, "if you lie to me one more time, you little—"

She saw me before they did, her wild dark eyes desperate in my direction.

Her cracked voice crying out, "Mister, mister!"

The one with the hand to her throat swiveled round, directing his little eyes on me. He had a thick brow, sloped nose, and square, steam shovel jaw. He squinted, anger momentarily befuddled—but he did not let go of the girl.

I asked him, "Got milk?"

"Wha—?"

Dropping my left shoulder, I swung the gallon jug up from behind my back. Momentum did the rest. The jug struck him full in the face, knocking him sidewise and one foot back. One of his teeth punctured the plastic, and the jug split wide open, bursting forth a torrent of calcium whitewash. He staggered on bowed legs, but didn't go over.

Drenched in milk, his nose bleeding freely, he shook his head and sprayed red and white drops. Hands clawed his face, not knowing what the liquid was. Then his eyes cleared beneath their soggy brows and they leveled on me. He looked like the sole survivor of a cow explosion.

I dropped the empty plastic container. A hollow, thin-shell *conk*. My heart was pounding me—I guess to beat the rush.

There was a gurgle and a giggling snort, then suddenly, from behind the milkman, his two partners burst into uncontrollable laughter.

He whirled and faced them. Whether from the blood in his eye or the actual stuff flowing from his nose, they shut up instantly.

I couldn't see the girl. I looked to my left. She was going up the steps to the sidewalk. She had the right idea. I followed. As soon as she hit pavement she was running. Me, I looked back.

They were right behind me, but had to come up the narrow steps one at a time.

Without thinking, I grabbed a lid off the nearest garbage can and swung it wild at the first one's head. But the lid *stuck* in mid-air, jerked outta my hand, and snapped back. It was chained to the railing.

The first man up dived at me in a tackle. We went back together, but didn't go down. My dress shoes had no traction, so I stayed standing, sliding upright until we collided into a parked car.

The collision knocked all my air out. I tried sucking some back, but couldn't.

Obvious truths, taken for granted, blaze like meteor streaks through the mind at times like these: You need *air* to breathe, *stupid*! And *I've lost her forever*. I even heard bells ringing.

Not bells, not ringing—wailing sirens, three distinct. I looked for the raspberry-and-cherry-swirl strobes of police cruisers converging, but the only flashing lights were the high beams of the vehicle we slumped against—our impact having triggered the car alarm.

The sound deluge—whooping, chirping, and eee-eee-eeeing at a stabbing pitch—didn't faze the Curlys one bit. Instead it seemed to drive them. Three pairs of hands grabbed and catapulted me to the ground. I landed on my left shoulder, the concussion rattling my teeth. It was a bad place to be, maybe the worst. I had to get up. I rolled over and pushed up with both my hands, then the first kick arrived.

Implanted in my kidney, the pain wedged in my left side like an ax blade, as another boot drove it, and another boot drove it, deeper and deeper in. Coring me.

I covered my back with my hands, and they kicked my head. I covered my head and they kicked at my chest, and at my balls, my arms, and my legs. I covered my balls and they kicked at my hands over my balls. It went on like that for five pages. I couldn't think of anything witty to say the whole time.

Part of me escaped into thoughts of Air—my nickname for Clair, my *pet* name for her, she'd say ("Just something to sigh when you're blue"). But she was that for me: cool, clear air. She used to call me Sure, a play on my last name, Sherwood, but no one calls me *that* anymore. What Clair's husband Brian calls her, I don't know, probably "early to bed." If we were still together, I thought, none of this would be happening. Well, at least not to me. In a way though, lying there, it gave me an opportunity to join in kicking.

The car alarm finished its cycle with a last chirp-chirp-iggy-bleep. The silence made my attackers pause. They were winded, huffing through dry mouths. Hard work beating a man, probably why so many do it in groups of two or more.

One gulped breath, and asked, "Hey, where'd she go?"

The milkman swore. Then swore down at me, using his boot for punctuation. Talk about your lactose intolerants.

One of the others said, "Stosh, come on, we gotta find her. Come on, man, there's a car turning at the light."

They went away then, I guess—didn't *know*, because every time I took a breath it felt like one was still kicking me. My cheek flat against the cool concrete, the eye I could still see out of focused on something freshly wet on the ground—Mercurochrome?

cherry syrup? my blood?—seeping out in a smooth, surfaceless stain, swallowing the glare of streetlight. A sheer, dizzying waste, whatever it was.

My vision went telescopic, my arm elongating, stretching out before me to what seemed like three blocks long, with my watch way way down at the end of it. I could still make out the time: five after two. I watched the thin hand passing the sluggish seconds, pain pulsating in unison. I closed my eye, but that hurt just as much.

When I opened it again, I saw her level with my gaze.

She hadn't run very far, only several yards to where a brown Jeep 4 × 4 was parked. She was crawling out from under it, the carriage just high enough for her to clear the granite curb.

From my perspective she was climbing out of a shaft into open space, in danger of falling, but then she just stuck straight out like a flagpole. Amazing. She walked over and crouched down beside me. I got my first good look at her then.

She was no more than sixteen. Her face as pale as loose-leaf, wide-ruled blue veins showing through. Her active eyes were hazel-brown trout trapped in shallow silty water. She chewed a loose skinflap off her lips as she leaned in closer to touch my hand.

Her fingers were rough and callused. Sticky. I smelled stronger her cloying scent of sweet patchouli as she started checking for my pulse. She had trouble finding one, so I made it easy on her.

" 'S okay," I said. "I'm live."

But she didn't stop fiddling with my wrist, actually started twisting it over the wrong way.

"Hey!" I said.

Her black, broken fingernails pried free the crown clasp of my gold Rolex, and the wristband unfolded. She dragged it off of me, scraping skin from my knuckles as it pulled free.

I grabbed her, but she just yanked from my grasp and started off in a shot, running away with my watch, straight toward Second

Avenue until she became as remote as its bright lights. Never looked back.

I had to get up. Go after her. I rolled over and pushed myself up. I got onto all fours before a queasy, eel-churning nausea yawned in me, and I felt myself going.

Out. Exactly like a light. The complete darkness.

Then you either wake up at the other end or don't.

I came to, knowing at first only who I was and not where or when in my life. It could've been the time my dad beaned me with a hardball playing catch in the backyard. Or when I fell eighteen feet from an elm tree while climbing a homemade rope ladder (always the things we're sure of that trip us up). Slowly, memory marched back and I remembered having been in a fight, but not, for the life of me, who or what I'd been fighting for. Then events stood at attention and I knew where I was again, and how I'd gotten there, but not who was speaking, harshly scolding me in a raspy foghorn drawl.

"Thas the problem, thas the problem, people lying around. Me, I got work to do, work to do."

My eyes opened to a rose hue, but at least I

could see out of both again. If I believed what I saw: a fuzzy blue house slipper tap-tapping the sidewalk in front of my face. Sprouting from it, a hairy, walnut-brown ankle growing up into a knobby knee. To see any more of him, I had to turn over.

The rest of his attire was equally elaborate: a peach-and-gold silk kimono worn beneath grass-stained football shoulder pads. He looked seven feet tall, his natty black hair standing straight up like a cornstalk, tied in place by a feather boa. His face was three shades darker than his ankles. Sweaty and concave, his sinister profile was quartermoon.

I recognized him, had known the man for ten years and never met or spoken a word to him. He was part of the East Village scenery I was used to seeing around, just a Technicolorful character in a neighborhood awash with colorful characters. I'd never had a reason to talk to him before.

He was leaning against a garland-strung grocery cart heaped with refuse—cordless appliances, water-warped paperbacks, unstuffed toys, and go-go boots—regarding me thoughtfully, shaking his feathered head, tsk-tsking.

"You're jus' wasting my time," he said, his craggy voice deeper than the subway subsewers. "I can't be standin' here talking to a man who jus' goin' waste my time when I got work to do and you're jus' wastin' my time."

He stalked about the sidewalk describing a square in long single strides. He found my box of Cheerios by the garbage cans, examined it, shook it, then put it on his cart. He came back, puzzled and miffed.

"You still here?"

I pled guilty.

"Thas no place to be. People always in the wrong place, wrong time."

"I hear ya."

"Hear me?! You better hear me!"—in a voice and volume impossible not to—"What ya going to *do* 'bout it?"

I lifted my arm. It bent in the right places. I propped myself up on an elbow, muscle grating against muscle, protesting movement, enlightening me with pain that snatched my breath and left me gasping and grinning.

"Whatcha cryin' for?"

I winced. "I'm an emotional guy."

I got myself into a sitting position and slumped there, catching my breath.

A little out of practice, I asked him, "Ahh, could . . . could you help me?"

He did a deliberate double take and flopped his hands to his sides. "What do you think I'm standin' here for? Didn't I jus' finish telling you I . . ." He gave up explaining to me in despair and disgust, tucked his hands under my armpits, and scooped me straight up. For a moment I was weightless, then sagged again. He lowered me down, my feet touching ground. And I hurt.

I hurt, I hurt, I hurt.

Did I mention I hurt.

Just then I hurt all over, but nothing like how I'd feel in the morning.

The man supported me as I took a step forward. He smelled thickly of cocoa butter and musky B.O. I hobbled to his cart and leaned. Using it as a kind of rolling walker, I took a tentative step forward.

"Do you mind if I . . . if I borrow your . . . I only live around the corner."

He craned back his neck and, for the very first time, looked at me—my face bloodied, my suit torn—with outright suspicion. He let go my arm.

"You don't live 'round here," he accused. "I know all the people who live around here and you don't live around here. What are you? You an outtatown-uptown, Wall Street–type lawyer out cruisin' for some ass?"

"No, really I—"

He shook his head. "No, no, I know the nayburrhood."

"Look, I'll show you where I live."

He mulled it over and kept mulling it as we inched our way toward Second Avenue.

Turning the corner, we met five late-night revelers, three men and two women all dressed funereal, falling over each other, laughing and screaming, screaming and laughing. They hardly looked our way, only a blip: an outrageously dressed black man and a white guy in a torn tailored suit pushing a cart full of trash. What's to notice?

We made our procession past the closed shops, a foot special-ist, a newsstand, the deli formerly the Chungs', the locksmith, and stopped at my building. I dug for keys.

"See," I said, unlocking the door. "I live here."

Unconvinced, he said resolutely, "I know the neighborhood and you're not from the neighborhood."

I couldn't argue with him—not then. I might lose. I reached in my pocket.

"Can I . . . ?"

He laughed a Harley backfire at the ten and two singles I held out, then he towed his cart away, shaking his head and reprimand-ing me with new vigor:

"Haven't I given you nuff my time? All this time I spent wastin' my time when I got work to do and you want to waste *more* of my time. Thas no way to be. No way."

I went inside; it was good to close a door behind me again.

The entryway was a cramped space with five mailboxes fitted into the wall, only three in use: mine, P. SHERWOOD INVESTIGA-TIONS; APERTURES, INC. (the photographer's studio I shared the second floor with); and, in the penthouse, TIGGER FITCHET, ACTIVIST.

Ahead rose the stairs to my door. Nine marble steps and then a landing, twelve steps and then a turn. Six more to the top. Mock-ing me. I started the climb and got the joke.

"Ow, ow. Ow."

Giddiness from blood loss, blind pain, or my appreciation for the ironic; whatever it was, on reaching the first landing I began to laugh. Hysterical giggles, really, echoing in the stairwell, as I trembled all over. The shakes went on long after I stopped laughing and was hanging from the banister, kneeling on the next step up.

I don't know how long I was like that, but after a while a metal door clanged above me, keys jangling, then heavy footsteps began clomping down the stairs.

A petite white woman appeared on the landing. She was dressed to go out in an olive-drab sweatshirt, plaid skirt, two pairs of torn fishnet stockings, and red high-tops with thick black-rubber soles. She froze when she saw me.

Her face registered the ancient instant dilemma of fight/flight before tightening into an animal snarl so fierce I almost didn't recognize her, not used to being on the receiving end of it. Also Tigger had shaved her head since I'd last seen her, and dyed the remaining nubbly fuzz chartreuse, her skull Day-Glo brilliant as a fresh yellow tennis ball.

She focused on me, as though through thinning mist, and slowly her features softened. Brown brows raised, golden-caramel eyes propped wide in alarm, the silver stud on her flaring nostril like a glob of stuck mercury. She gaped.

"Holy shit, Payton, did you get hit by a cab?"

I gave a healthy laugh, grateful. Grateful to be home, grateful to be alive, grateful to have someone taking over the gag lines. I felt safe enough to pass out again.

I woke up on the couch in my apartment, a sopping towel of ice cubes on my face. I peeked out. Tigger, beside me, was bandaging a long, shallow cut on my side. She must have lugged me the rest of the way up. Not her first time hauling an inert body.

I relaxed in her hands. In the time I'd know her, Tigger had survived more than her share of police actions, squatter evictions, ri-
ots, and other last stands ending either in tear gas or the flail of
black batons. She knew all about treating the walking wounded.

I jolted as she splashed on alcohol. Her bedside manner could
stand improvement.

"So you're back," she said.

I sucked in through my teeth. "Do you mean in the city or
amongst the living?"

"What the hell happened?"

A good question. I wished I had a better answer for her than
the truth. "I was stupid."

She sat down in a chair and listened, arranging and rearranging
her legs beneath her, sometimes perching or tucking in a knee,
but constantly squirming. Her expression pooled into appalled
disbelief. She squinted her eyes, trying to visualize what I was
telling her. When I got to the part where they started putting in the
boot, she put her own feet down, and stopped me—wouldn't let
me go on—shouting, "I can't believe you!"

"Well, at the time—"

"When did all this happen? When did you even get back?"

"Oh, about . . ." I checked my watch, or tried to, instead staring
stupidly at my naked wrist. "Oh, yeah," I said, "and then the girl
came back and stole my Rolex."

Tigger looked surprised. "You have a Rolex?"

"Had. I got it last year from a jeweler in lieu of payment for
arranging his security at a monthlong trade show. But I never
wear it."

"Well, that makes sense."

I was still looking at where my watch had been, at the white
band of untanned skin. In the morning, I'd have to put on my
regular wristwatch again, the durable, black, nylon-strapped,
luminous-dial camper I wore on the job.

I asked her, "Think I should report it?"

"You must be joking," Tigger said. "It wasn't insured, was it? Then you'd be wasting your time."

I smiled. "That's what the guy who helped me home told me. You know, that tall streetguy with the real froggy voice who's always—"

"Calvin? *Calvin* helped you?" She shook her head. "Man, you must've looked pathetic to get his attention."

It figured Tigger knew him.

Something occurred to her and she swore under her breath. She went over to my phone, started punching in numbers.

"What's up?"

"Ez is at Twilo tonight, filling in for the regular DJ mixing the house. I told him I'd come by."

"It's almost three now," I pointed out, the soused den mother sprawled out on the daybed spouting virtue.

"That's okay," she said. "I'll just beep him I'll be late."

"Don't bother. I'm fine."

"You sure?"

I grunted, sitting up. "Just help me get to the bathroom."

I leaned on her and she guided me.

"You've got a deep cut over your eye," she said. "It may need stitches. I cleaned and bandaged it. Looks like it stopped bleeding though."

When we reached the bathroom door, she let go. I didn't fall. Spectacular.

"Thanks," I said, gripping the door frame. "And for the ice cubes."

"I'll knock when I get home, to make sure you haven't lapsed into a coma. I mean, seriously, you could have a concussion."

"I'll keep it in mind." It sounded like a bad pun. I laughed. Maybe I did have a concussion. Tigger gave me a worried frown.

"Just go," I told her. "I'll be okay."

At the door she turned back, her face in a stern deadpan of disapproval. "Try not to do anything else dumb tonight, will ya?"

I waved her away, then hobbled into the bathroom. I passed by the mirror without daring to look in.

Pissing hurt like hell, but I was relieved to see my urine only came out a pale chamomile. I needed to eat more vegetables, sure, but at least I wasn't bleeding internally. I flushed and went over to the mirror.

At the best of times, I've seen only a stranger looking back at me. Sometimes, a someone I wouldn't mind getting to know, other times someone I wouldn't have made eye contact with under any other circumstances. But the face I sought recognition in at that moment only invited pity.

"Look what you've done to yourself," I said.

"I know, I know. I had help."

The white gauze square taped over my left eye was dotted red, but not wet where I touched. Below it, a developing welt on my cheek was puffy, jaundiced purple, the skin waxy and unreal. I felt it. "Ouch."

I asked, "Does it hurt in there? It hurts out here."

I nodded, then undressed and looked at myself naked. I used to pose nude for Clair, when she was an artist, before she got married. She always painted me better than I was—that was her crime. But she taught me to see things I'd only thought I saw before, great for work. I learned to sketch with the negative-space technique: drawing the shapes around a form, instead of the object itself. For instance, I had a bunch of bananas under each arm.

The really funny thing, though, was that while looking over my battered body—the wreckage both new and old, fresh wounds and old ones reopened—my gaze fell first and foremost on my left wrist and the band of negative-tan there. Like a pink bracelet and a void.

I lit a cigarette and smoked. I put on a fresh pair of boxers and got into bed. I wanted sleep more than anything.

I didn't want to lie there aching, staring at the back of my eyelids, watching the incident on Eleventh Street replay in my mind, looping over and over again, while I tried to edit it in motion, cutting what I did and splicing in what I should've done.

An hour went by. Sixty-nine minutes passed.

I was angry at myself, playing this kind of fruitless game I used to as a kid. You can't change the past by worrying it endlessly through your imagination.

But still it persisted, wouldn't let up, my heart reacting as vividly as if it were happening all over again for the first time, my emotions unable to separate the real from the imagined. My body glazed over in a cold-jelly sweat. I rolled back and forth, binding myself in covers. Accept it and forget it, I raged at myself. Not for the first time.

But accepting loss has never been my strong suit.

So finally, in order to get some rest, I hired myself, took on my restless soul as a client, promising him, "In the morning, I'll succeed in getting it all back for you, everything you've lost: your life, your love, your city. Or at the very least, your watch."

After that, I slept like a cat, deep in mouse dreams.

Bright morning glare slashed a paper cut across my eyes. The rest of me wasn't so hot either. I got up with every cliché of pain I could think of, groaned with every breath, lit a cigarette, and smoked. Made black coffee and drank.

Opposite my window, the dentist on the second floor in the facing building dug into his patient's mouth with a glinting silver probe.

I drained the sugary residue from my cup of black coffee and shuddered. It was ten A.M. Friday. I needed milk.

The first step involved leaving the apartment. Trickier than it sounds: I still had to dress and my range of motion was severely limited. I was pain-dazzled putting on my blue jeans. Unable to face buttons or laces, I wormed my body into an extra-large sweatshirt and my bare feet into soft brown-leather brogues. A pair of sunglasses and I was off.

Out the street door I went left, the way I had last night, turning onto East Twelfth. People seemed to zoom by me as I shuffled along. An Asian woman wearing silver spandex and lime-green Rollerblades. Two men with briefcases sharing a cellular phone. A Caribbean nanny pushing two blonde, blue-eyed children in a twin-seat stroller. A pensioner struggling with groceries. Each could've lapped me twice-round-the-block.

It gave me time to think.

When I reached the deli on Third Avenue, I walked in and went over to the milk cooler. This time I only got a quart. Issuing small arms.

The Hindu clerk looked up from pricing vitamins at the counter and his eyes widened. I was no pretty picture, but since he didn't know me he didn't say anything, only rang up my milk and bagged it.

If he wasn't going to ask me, I guessed I'd have to tell him. So, as conversationally as I could, I related what had happened, watering it down to a mugging, and giving a description of the four involved, the girl and the three stooges, one named Stosh.

"Seen anyone around like that?"

Silently, he shook his head no. Which was a lie of sorts. There was a young skinhead studying the Hostess Twinkies rack behind me who could've been any one of the three—same build and kick-ass demeanor—only he wasn't. What the clerk really meant was, it wasn't any of his business. It was going to be like that everywhere I went.

I thanked him, but he just stared. I'd have to come back and ask the night man. "Poke into every hollow," my old boss Matt Chadinsky used to say.

I stepped outside and turned left, walking to the corner of East Eleventh.

The three stooges hadn't grabbed the girl at random. They knew her and had been waiting for her to pass by. Where had she been coming from?

Across the two-way traffic of Third Avenue, the northwest corner housed a seven-level movieplex and the southwest, a sushi bar. On my side, the opposite corner was a stationery store, and the corner I stood on, the NYU off-campus dorm.

A lot of activity outside it that morning, families retrieving graduating seniors. Vans, station wagons, and U-Haul trucks were doubled-parked along the street. Two women, mother and daughter, carried a microwave oven between them. A young man in shorts hefted a milk crate packed with textbooks into the trunk of a BMW.

The girl last night had looked too young to be in college, I thought, or maybe I was simply too old to differentiate any longer. But before she'd taken my watch, I'd touched her hands, callused and sticky, not the hands of a student living in a comfortable dormitory, more like the hands of a street kid, used to hugging pavement and entreating spare change.

Still a possibility though, but pointless to go to the front desk and ask. Looking as I did I'd have security on me in a flash.

I continued down Eleventh, back in the direction of Second Avenue, passing four ornamental pear trees, blossoming with white flowers like popcorn balls I hadn't noticed the night before. I was doing all I could do, going back over the ground, retracing my steps, looking without knowing what I was looking for. Anything that might lead me to the girl. But she'd be hiding now, since others were looking, too, others who had a distinct advantage: they knew where to look. My only edge was, the girl didn't know I was after her. Fat lotta good it did me, too.

In the bright of day, the shadowy places illuminated, all the distances seemed shorter.

The cars parked along the street were still bumper to bumper. I stopped where I'd first noticed her coming out from behind an elm tree, oddly leafless that late in spring. I looked around the tree trunk and by the curb for anything she might've dropped, but there was nothing around but the broken glass of green and brown beer bottles.

I shuffled farther along, fixing my eyes before my feet, scanning the cracked and buckled concrete. Mended in spots, names etched in the hardened cement. A child's handprint, a smile face.

Clues literally littered the ground—a matchbook with a penciled phone number, a lost car-key case, an inside-out purse, a lipstick-smeared Newport cigarette butt, a hair scrunchy with snagged strands of blonde extensions. Nothing recent though; all were weatherworn and gritty.

It was impossible to miss the spot I got stomped, marked by my own blood dried dark brown and queerly enameled. I tried not to look at it, but the congealed smear had a magnetic pull. Blood calling to blood. I thought I was supposed to be desensitized to gore by movies and nightly news, but I still felt the earth slip, skipping over a worn-down cog in its gradual spinning. I forced myself to concentrate on the surrounding ground, but still didn't find anything useful.

One last place to check: I crossed to the semibasement entryway. I glanced up and down the street before I went down. Across the street at the rear gate of St. Mark's churchyard, a redheaded Hispanic woman was leading a flock of first-graders by a towrope with dozens of little handles. I descended.

The subground patio was cluttered with trash. Soda cups, yellowed newspapers, a half-dozen used condoms, dried up like the shed skin of snakes. Under the iron staircase, the puddle of milk was a solid curdle. I tried not to step in it or on the confusion of white bootprints as I looked the area over. The sour smell was oppressive and reminded me of my junior-high cafeteria and drinking lukewarm half-pints.

I didn't find a damn thing. I didn't expect to, but you hope. As I

started back up the crumbling steps to the sidewalk, the hopeless-
ness sank in. I didn't have anything.

The church clock began to sound the hour, eleven, tolling to
me that I should've *known* . . . should've *known* . . . should've
known . . .

On the way home, I walked by the Jeep 4 × 4 the girl had
crawled out from under; it was still parked in the same spot. Then
I stopped, took a step back. "Poke into every hollow."

Bracing myself by the door handle, I knelt beside it and eyed
the refuse along the curb in front of the 4 × 4. We're all in the
gutter, I thought, but some of us are looking at the swollen cigarette ends, wadded pizza-parlor napkins, and a discarded, tooth-
less comb. I stooped even lower and looked underneath.

I saw something small and black about a foot in beneath the
Jeep. I had to lie flat on my bruised ribs and endure shock waves
of pain to reach it. A small rectangular object that fit snug in the
palm of my hand.

I looked at it, a cheap knockoff pager, its face scraped, the
service-provider name scratched out with a pin. On the back of
it, an empty slot where a missing belt clip slid in; it could've
easily come apart when the girl crawled out. I looked at the liquid-
crystal display on top, a thin digital readout. The beeper was
still switched on; it hadn't been there long enough for the batteries to run down. I pushed a small red button on the front and the
screen displayed the last number received, the number before
that, and two more stored in the beeper's memory. I kissed the
damn thing.

When I got back to my office the answering machine flashed a
tenth message. I still hadn't checked the first nine. After I put
away the milk, I sat down and pushed PLAY, listening to them as I
copied down the numbers stored inside the beeper.

Half-a-dozen messages began cordially enough: "Mr. Payton
Sherwood, you have until midnight tonight to contact our

Citibank Visa offices regarding a *vital* matter"—followed by an 800 number. Each received on a different day.

Two messages were from my mom thanking me for the cachepot of geraniums I'd sent her for Mother's Day.

One message was from Matt Chadinsky, part owner of Metro Security and Surveillance, Inc., where I'd served a five-year apprenticeship before striking out on my own. *Striking out* was right.

"Hey, Pay, got some work for you this weekend, if you aren't too swamped." He laughed. "We need an extra man at a wedding reception out on Long Island. To blend in with the guests, keep an eye on the gifts, and keep out the gate-crashers. Ya get to wear a tux! Nice fee, little work, free food. Maybe even pick up a bridesmaid. Call me."

Swell, and me looking like squashed pigeon.

The last was from Tigger.

"Hey, you there? Pick up. I knocked but no answer. You okay? Hello? It's ten-thirty. I'll be up for another hour. Don't make me call fire-and-rescue."

I called her back first, woke her. Cranky.

"Didn't you hear me kicking the door?" she slurred.

"I had to go out."

"Howya feeling today?"

"Like a million bucks. In small, crumpled bills."

She giggled, murmuring more comfortably, "But you're alive?"

"I'll let you know. What time you go to work?"

"We've got a seven o'clock call, be in at six-thirty."

"Can I pick your brain later? Over coffee?"

"Brain-and-brain, what is *brain*?!"

"Huh?"

"Nuthin'." She yawned. "Ez dubbed some *Star Trek* samples into his mix last night. 'Spock's Brain Is Missing.' I can't get them outta my head."

"I'll give you the Vulcan mind-meld. 'Round four?"

"I'll call *you* after five."

"Goodnight."

"G'mornin'."

I heard her stretch and moan sleepily as she fumbled the receiver back into its cradle.

I hung up, then rang Metro Security and Surveillance, and asked the receptionist—a new man whose voice I didn't recognize—for Matt Chadinsky.

"What name, sir?"

"Nando Shmocki."

"Please hold, Mr. Shmocki."

A few bars of "Isn't She Lovely?" later.

"Nando *Shmocki*," Matt said. "Where'd you come up with that?"

"It was the court reporter's name in Syracuse."

"You're shittin' me. How'd that go?"

"We lost. Motherhood prevailed."

"Can't beat that. So, Pay, 'bout this wedding. I need you to—"

"Uh . . ."

"Whadya mean, '*uh*'? You're not passin' on this? You must be shittin' me."

I assured him I wasn't, told him what had happened, how I now looked.

"Are you shittin' me?"

"Matt, I really wish I was."

"Damn," he said. "I was counting on you."

Not the best time to ask for a favor, but I plowed on. "Get me addresses on some local numbers?" I asked.

"Can't be in that bad a shape, working something."

He still didn't half believe me, thought I was just blowing off the security work because it was beneath me (a notion he'd gotten into his head when I quit). I gave him the rest, about finding the beeper, and my hopes of tracing the girl through it and getting back my watch.

Issuing no comment on my dubious motives, Matt chewed it over professionally.

"Too bad no service's name. Probably some cheap outfit you coulda got her name out of. Doubt she even has an address. Sounds street."

"Yeah, so how about the help?"

He groaned, shuffled papers in front of the phone. "Give me the numbers. I'll bill you on a sliding scale."

"Good luck sliding that far, you'll hurt yourself. Jeanne'd never forgive me."

I read him the four phone numbers. He said he'd fax me the results.

"Thanks."

"Whatcha going to do with them once you get 'em?"

I totally misunderstood him for a second, thought he meant the three guys who beat me. Flash pictures of scouring their white faces against stucco pleased me, until I realized Matt was talking about the addresses.

"Well, I figure, if other people're looking for her, I can contact them and . . ." I trailed off; that was about as far as I'd gotten.

"And what, Pay, form a club? You watch too much fucking TV. Gimme an hour." He hung up.

I sat there, not knowing for a couple minutes I was staring down at the phone.

I probably should've cut my losses. My gold Rolex was long gone anyhow, most likely traded for drugs or the money to buy drugs. By the light of day, I didn't even blame the girl for taking it, me lying there such easy pickings. And as for the three gentlemen, well, karma could sort them out.

But I knew I wouldn't leave it alone—couldn't drop it. Hell, I was still daydreaming about a woman I hadn't seen in five years, a year longer than we were even together.

I tried again to read a name off the scratched face of the beeper, tilting it back and forth under the desk lamp to catch the glare when it suddenly came alive in my hand, twitching and squirming like a fidgety black beetle. I dropped it.

It landed on a pile of my unpaid credit card bills, a past-due notice for my last Oxford Health premium, and a cutoff warning from Time Warner Cable. It slid a little, quivering, shifting my mound of debt. It purred like an electric razor.

The beeper was set for vibrate; a call was coming in. I picked it up again. On the thin screen, a seven-digit number appeared. Not one of the ones I'd given to Matt.

Without thinking—phone already to my ear—I dialed the number; too late once the connection was made, it picked up on the second ring.

A woman's nasally voice sweetly answered, "Lower Eastside Veterinary Hospital."

"Hi, returning your page."

"Um."

She'd paged a woman and a man answered. It confused her. In the background a dog yipe-yipe-yiped. She said, "I'm sorry, I'm trying to get someone else."

"Yeah, she's busy right now, asked me to check."

"Gloria Manlow?"

"Right. Is it about her dog?" I asked.

Just a guess, but what other kind of pet would a street kid have—a cat? a turtle? a marmoset?

"Yes," the woman said. "Ms. Manlow told us she'd pick him up this morning at ten. Is she on her way?"

"I don't know."

"Well, please tell her if she doesn't pick up Pike by noon, we'll have to charge her another day's board. On top of the three days already, and the balance she currently owes on his surgery . . ." Her voice got trebly.

"How's Pike doing?" I asked, more to keep the conversation flowing.

"He's healing well. He'd be a lot better if she came and got him. Tell her if it's because of her bill, we can work out a payment plan. But she really must—"

"How much does she owe?"

"Three hundred sixty-five dollars. Three eighty-five if she doesn't come this morning. We can only board him for a week. It's been three days now."

"Then what happens?"

"We turn him over to the ASPCA."

"I'll let her know," I said. "How long she been bringing Pike to you?"

"It has nothing to do with her being a new client. Anyone—if we can't contact the owner in a certain time—I mean, we're not a kennel."

I said, "I'm sure it's not something you want to do."

"It's great that these kids adopt these pound-strays, but, I mean, please, they're strays themselves, you know? Can barely support themselves."

"What kind of surgery was it?"

"He'd been stabbed with a broken bottle. Some of his leg muscles had to be reattached. I thought you were a friend of hers?"

"I've been out of town." I didn't push my luck. I just thanked her and said I'd pass on the message.

After I hung up, I caught myself staring at the phone again. I was becoming a champion phone-starer. I got out the white pages and looked up the animal hospital in the business listings and wrote down the address: 76 East Third Street.

I pushed back my chair and started to rise, but only got a half inch before pain rooted me back to the spot. Too long in one place, my body had stiffened, raw muscles issuing severe warnings—commands, really—against any movement at all. Well, fuck that.

Breathless, I hugged my ribs and crouched forward, resting my head on the desk. I braced my hands and eased weight onto my legs. Crooked as with osteoporosis, I got myself out of the chair and onto my feet.

Pain seized me again as I took a step forward, blinding me with TV snow as I fought back a lightness like falling. When it finally cleared, I was still on my feet.

"Progress," I urged, and took another painful step, well on my way.

I could've taken a cab, but didn't trust being able to get out of it again. I only had to travel nine blocks. Walking at my present rate, I might've made it by Tuesday. At the bus stop in front of my building, I looked left to the oncoming traffic of cars and vans, a limo and a cement truck. Far up Second Avenue rose the white crest of a bus roof. I fished out a token and waited with it in my hand.

I'd discovered her name. Gloria Manlow. She would've had to fill out an admission form for her dog at the vet's. Given some sort of address. I had to see it. Any chance of her showing up while I was there I jinxed simply by wishing it'd be that easy.

A great white whale, the bus, veered to the

curb and stopped abruptly. An M15 local to City Hall. Five other passengers seated onboard. I rode standing, gripping a steel loop, reading an overhead advertisement for hemorrhoidal laser surgery and a Langston Hughes poem about loss (or what I thought it was about). I signaled my stop.

The building numbers ascended evenly as I walked along the south side of Third Street, past two art galleries and a Jamaican music store. Most of the block was composed of gray stone and brick apartment houses with dingy tiled entryways. Number 76 was located directly across the street from the NYC headquarters of Hell's Angels. Out front, six fat Harleys slouched in a row like soldiers at ease. No activity this early, not yet noon.

I abandoned the idea of staking out the vet's. It was a bad vicinity to aimlessly loiter, especially looking like I'd been in one fight already. It wasn't likely the girl would come for her dog that day anyway, not if she was lying low. But you never know.

From the outside, the animal hospital looked like a plant store, flowering window boxes and several tall ferns in planters chained to an ironwork fence. A hand-painted sign hung over the door: HOURS BY APPOINTMENT. The door was oak with a brass handle and six glass panels, a sticker on one: PETS NEED DENTAL CARE, TOO.

I pushed the bell and the latch clacked. I went in. The reception area had terra-cotta flooring and lacquered pine benches. Only one patient waiting—a lady with a plastic carry-kennel, white whiskers peeking out its grille. I crossed over to the receptionist touch-typing on a curved, ergonomic keypad. After a solid minute she looked up at me.

She was a young, fresh-faced strawberry blonde. Solid forehead and a small pink-painted mouth. Her bland expression made nothing of my bruised face. Maybe she'd seen worse, working on the Lower East Side. I know I had.

"Yes?"

"Hi, I'm a friend of Gloria's. We spoke on the phone. About Pike."

Her blue eyes were neutral. "Yes?"

"I wasn't able to talk to her yet, and was wondering if she called?"

She shook her head.

The bell rang and she buzzed the door latch. It opened and a tall woman entered holding taut the leash of a slender gray husky with glacier-green eyes. The dog sniffed at the carry-kennel on the bench and the cage hopped to one side like a jumping bean.

The tall woman yanked the dog leash, saying, "No, Nanette, no! Goooood girl."

I resumed my pitch to the receptionist.

"I think Gloria's strapped for cash right now," I told her, "and she won't admit it. I don't want anything to happen to her dog meantime."

I pulled out my wallet and looked inside. A creased twenty and a single. On the countertop, decals for three major credit cards. My Visa card doubtful, I slid over Discover. "Could I get a look at her bill? See how much I can handle."

She smiled at me. Now I was a customer. Her fingers clicked over the keyboard as she summoned the information to her screen.

She said, "Usually we refer these kids over to the ASPCA or a clinic. For minor problems, you know, spaying, neutering, shots. But her dog's leg was badly torn. Seventeen stitches. Little thing, too, thirty-two pounds. Oh, you don't have to lean. I'll print it up. How much did you want to pay on the three-eight-five balance?"

I figured the cost and profit of information. "A hundred twenty dollars."

She typed in the amount and slid my card through a sensor. We waited a tense ninety seconds to see if it would clear. I heard the *Jeopardy* theme in my head.

A receipt began to print out. I signed it and got back my plastic. She swiveled her chair over to the printer and rolled back

again with two sheets. She handed them to me, but then held on
with a little tug. I didn't tug back.

I met her steady gaze. Blue, blue eyes, even her whites a Dres-
den china blue.

"Would you like to see him?" she asked me.

"Who?"

"Pike. He could stand the attention."

"Oh, yeah. Sure."

She let go of the papers in my hand. I didn't even look, just
folded them and put them in my pocket, and followed her round
the counter to a rear door of glass and chicken-wire mesh. As the
door opened, an animal aroma hit me—hot, funky, sour—and a
discordant wail of woofs, mraows, and clucking calls. The cement
floor was tacky with antiseptic. The cages, about twenty in all,
were built the length of both walls. Some were small enough for
rabbits, a couple big enough to fit Saint Bernards. Located in a
middle row, one down from a bug-eyed Chihuahua in a neck
brace, was Pike's medium-sized cage.

Pike was sitting in a back corner amongst newspaper scraps,
crouched in on himself, gargoylish. He was all skin and muscle, a
honey-colored pit bull with big white paws and a pink-white
snout with gray whiskers, made ridiculous by an off-white plastic
cone—like an upside-down lampshade—around his neck to prevent him from biting his stitches.

"Hey, boy," I said.

He rolled his eyes desolately, his rat tail curled motionless
round his hind legs.

The receptionist silently watched me.

"Come here, Pike. Come 'ere, boy."

I lifted my hand to the bars—and stopped. It was a pit bull.

Hesitantly, I poked two bare fingers in. The dog rose on all legs
and crossed in a side-to-side bound. His hot nose touched my
hand and he sniffed long and hard at my skin, comparing its scent

against his private catalog of past offenders. Feeling his steamy
breath, I had to hook my fingers on the cage to keep from yanking
them out. His mouth cracked open in a slavering grin of crocodile
teeth. His tongue lolled and licked my hand. Turning his head
sidewise, he brushed my fingers with a velvet-soft and floppy ear.

Obediently, I scratched him, saying, "Good dog. Good boy,
Pike."

I meant it.

"Does he get exercised?" I asked.

"Some. But a dog like this, he's used to roaming around, doesn't
understand being cooped up all day. Remind his owner of that
when you see her."

"If I see her. She forgot her beeper at my place and now I'm
having trouble getting ahold of her."

"Oh?"

I stopped scratching Pike and he eyed me like "Where ya
goin'?"

I took out a notepad and wrote down my first name and phone
number. I tore the page off and handed it to her. "If you hear from
her, I'd appreciate you giving me a call," I said. "And if you don't,
well . . . call me before they do anything about Pike."

I put my hands up to the bars and scratched again at both his
ears. His plastic collar balked against the cage door. He looked
like a *Looney Tunes* pup with its head stuck inside a funnel.

"I got to go now," I told him. "Gotta find your moms."

I walked away, turned back. His brown eyes, from behind bars,
were baffled and betrayed.

I thanked the receptionist for her help. She handed me her business card. ROXANNE PIETRA, *MEDICAL SECRETARY*. I stood corrected.

"Thanks again, Roxanne."

She crinkled the skin around her eyes, then reached a hand up
to my left temple. I almost shied away, but she only touched my
forehead gently and smoothed down a curled-up corner of the
bandage over my eye. Something puzzled her; her blue-blue eyes

wondered it in mine, until the phone rang and she had to answer that first. She said, "Well, good luck anyway, Payton."

A little unsettling. When you're a dweller in the woodwork by profession, it isn't always pleasant getting noticed. This was different though. I got out of there, my ego still on hunger strike.

Outside, I read over the billing information I'd paid $120 to get a look at, at first glance not worth even half that. It itemized the cost of Pike's surgery, anesthesia, and three days' food and boarding. He'd been admitted Tuesday at nine A.M. Badly wounded, shards of glass removed. Sex, color, and markings were listed. Eleven months old, a mixed breed, pit bull and boxer.

In the space for "owner" was Gloria's name, the 917 prefixed number to her beeper, and an address farther east, in Alphabet City. No apartment number.

I crossed the street and headed east. Turning the corner of First Avenue, I almost bumped into a carrot-topped man in a black turtleneck removing the padlocks on the gates of Little Rickie's gift emporium, its windows crowded with tchotchkes—a buxom Bettie Page wall clock, sharp-edged metal wind-up toys, 3-D postcards of Jesus Christ, a plaster headbust of Elvis, rubber crocodiles, and a stack of Ganesha lunchboxes.

During a lull in traffic, I cut across the erratic five lanes of First Avenue. But hobbling badly—or too well—I took longer than the lull, and had to dodge out of the way of a speeding FedEx truck. I stumbled over the curb, and a nasty twinge crept up my right leg and sank incisors deep into my lower back. I needed a cigarette, or an aspirin, or both.

The address Gloria had given was 729 East Ninth Street, six streets up and at least three avenues over, maybe four. Either way, I couldn't walk it, so I flagged a cab.

When I asked the driver if I could smoke in his cab, he said no. I got in anyway.

He raced us up First Avenue and swung east onto Sixth Street, then sped past Avenues A and B. Nearing C, or Loisaida Avenue, we entered a Latino barrio. Tenements. Vacant lots, ignored by the city, claimed by the residents for parking lots and community gardens. On the crumbling walls, giant murals of sports stars, superheroes, mythical beasts (unicorns and the Minotaur) in a rainbow of spray paints.

Slower going here, cars and pickups double-parked. At Avenue D, we turned uptown. Ahead on Fourteenth, the brick stacks of the Con Edison electrical plant stood high like a row of dormant silos. To the right, over the FDR Drive and the crinkled-lead surface of the East River, was a neon Domino Sugar sign facing out from Brooklyn. The cabbie turned onto Ninth Street.

The north-corner building was under construction. Blue scaffolding, splotched with cement, surrounded it. On the south side of the street was another project under way, courtesy of the Department of Housing Preservation and Development. Four-story sandstone buildings, low-income housing that from the outside looked like one-room schoolhouses. Many of the new windows still had manufacturer names pasted on them; some had already been smashed. Two hard-hatted workers, pushing around wheelbarrows full of bricks, eyed my cab suspiciously, or I'm paranoid, or both.

Farther along, the street was desolate. It seemed a waste of the cab fare—not to mention the $120—when I got to the approximate address, a line of fenced-in lots, one of which was a private parking area. The nearest actual building was a derelict five-story brownstone surrounded on all sides by rubble. The fire-blackened entrance was boarded up; its painted numerals, 737, were barely visible.

Where number 729 should've been was a chain-link fence enclosing a green garden with flowering paths, trees, and shrubs. I had the cabbie stop.

Inside the garden, a man was using a broken-handled hoe to scoop peat moss from a twenty-pound bag sitting inside a three-wheeled grocery cart. He spread it out over sandy topsoil. He was viper thin, dressed in loose denim from head to ankle, a blue-jean slouch hat pulled down low over long, gunky black-silver hair and orange-tinted sunglasses. A black Fu Manchu mustache was pasted down his hollow cheeks like a cheap disguise.

Because of his shades, I couldn't tell whether he saw me getting out of the cab or not, but he began tilling the earth farther down the lot, and by the time I crossed the pavement to the fence, he was at the door of a toolshed built against the rear wall of an abandoned building the next street over. I called out, but he shut the door behind him.

The shack was constructed of scrapwood, cardboard, sections of billboard, and broken street signs, like DO NOT ENTER and ONE WAY.

I tried the gate. Padlocked, a motorcycle chain coiled twice around. I gazed over the garden. Not often you got to admire nature in the city and, strangely, so far into its ruins. A gathering of daisies and a row of shrubs ran along a curving path paved with flagstone slivers, potsherds, and broken bricks squarely embedded in the earth. Peeking from behind the variety of flora were chipped lawn sculptures of a Ukrainian eagle, a bearded gnome, and a blue-stained Madonna.

I limped back to the cab and eased myself in. The cabbie's black-rimmed eyes studied me intently in the rectangle of rearview mirror. Where to?

I might have known the address'd be a phony. A waste of my time and my money. Well, my good credit. The spending of future funds, like I was bailing water *into* my sinking ship. Rowboat, life raft, whatever. The cab there and home again robbed me of eight more of my twenty-one remaining bucks.

My resolve began to dissolve now that my quest was starting to cost me.

When I got in the apartment, the faxes from Matt were waiting for me in the tray. And one new message on my answering machine.

I lit up a cigarette, and then played the message. I thought it'd be Matt checking that I got his fax. But it was someone who wanted to hire me. Of all things.

A Suffolk County attorney with a high, chuckly voice and too much divorce work on hand who said a satisfied client had recommended me. I couldn't imagine. He left his number.

I hated marital investigations, which is sort of like saying I hated paying the rent. I hated paying the rent.

I overdid my limping, not getting back to the machine in time to save the message before it rewound.

What did I want work for anyway? I had a hobby.

CHAPTER 5

I read the cover sheet from Matt. He'd only gotten two hits out of four. Of the two he couldn't find, one was a public pay phone south of East Fourteenth Street (location based only on the exchange). The second was a cellular phone, untraceable, its service Maximocom, a high-security telecommunications operation with the latest digital signal-scrambling technology. Not cheap, something like a dollar a minute per local call. Wherever, whoever, it connected to, it connected to money.

The second fax sheet was a printout of all four numbers and their results, listed as they'd appeared on the beeper, in the reverse order received, the last first.

1. Pay phone number.
2. Digital phone number.
3. Residence listed to Theodore Wylie, 617 East Eleventh, #9.
4. Business listed to Powers Orloff, 93 Van Brunt Street, Brooklyn.

The information looked pretty scant alone on the page. Whether to make something more of it or exhaust the possibilities as soon as possible, I began dialing the numbers one after the other.

The first one rang and rang; it was the pay phone, so I let it. I counted the rings up to twelve before my mind wandered off on its own. My big arched windows, like wide-open eyes in a huge cartoon head facing northeast, badly needed washing, the slant of noonday sun making opaque the streaked coating of pollen, pollution, and grime.

"Oy? Bon día."

I came to. On the line, tinny samba music was in the background. No sound of traffic. I said hello and started to say more.

"No open café." His accent a cross between Spanish and Italian.

"Where—"

"Open one clock."

I wracked my brain for some high school Spanish. No luck, I took French. "Location . . . locale . . . uh . . ."

"Ah, sim! Sim! *Avenida* A *y* . . . ten!"

"Thanks, um, *gracias.*"

"De nada."

Under the pay phone's number I wrote, *Café—Tenth and A.*

I dialed the second number, the digital phone. The line was busy; an automatic message invited me to please try my call again later. I put a question mark next to it.

I dialed the phone number listed to Theodore Wylie. Pessimist that I am, I didn't expect an answer, so wasn't disappointed. No answering machine; it rang for two minutes before I gave up.

I tried the last number. Powers Orloff in Brooklyn.

It rang twice then double-clicked, and a throaty female voice answered, "Hello?"—the subdued hello of someone coming off call-waiting. She was on the other line.

"Hi," I said. "I'm calling for Gloria Manlow."

"Gloria? Who—oh, you mean Glo? Everyone's looking. She's not here now." Her voice was sultry and hoarse, like she'd laughed too long and hard as a child.

"When would be a good time to catch her?"

"Dunno, she's suppose to be sitting for Pow at four, but yester—hey, who is this?"

"I'm calling from the Lower Eastside Veterinary Hot spittle—Hos-pital. It's about her dog." That should've come out smoother, but I'd had a rough night.

"What're you talking about? Glo doesn't have a dog. Is this *Teddy*?" She laced the name generously with Freon.

"No, I—"

"Yeah, yeah. Listen, just leave her alone," she said. "It's over. Get it?"

Misdirected as it was, it still struck close to home. I sputtered, "Please, could—"

She broke the connection.

I didn't call back. Wrote under the Brooklyn address: *4:00 Baby-sitting???* Farther up the list, next to the name Theodore Wylie, I jotted down, *Teddy. Ex?* It filled out the page nicely.

I dialed the cell phone number again and this time it rang.

"Hey-yo," a young man's voice lazily singsonged following a soft bleep. In the background, loud, sharp-edged music crashed like bags of glass flung down fire stairs.

"Yeah, hey, hi," I said. "Glo there?"

"Glo?"

The techno-metal music dropped ten decibels. A second voice, anxious in the background, asked, "Is that Glo? That her? Let me talk to her, let me—"

The mouthpiece was muffled.

"Who's this?" a voice asked, still the same lazy one that first answered.

"I'm trying to get ahold of Glo."

"She's not here."

"Oh man," I said. "I've gotta split this afternoon and she left her stuff here."

"Who's this?"

"Payton. This Teddy?"

"No, you a friend of Ted's?"

"No, but I thought they were together."

"No more," he droned. "They broke up."

"Wow, guess that's why she gave me this number."

"Did you try beeping her?"

"Yeah, but no answer so far."

"Well, still kinda early, y'know."

"Yeah, I know, I'm just worried with those guys jumping her last night and—"

"What?" For the first time, a measure of interest.

The second voice echoed urgently, "What? *What?*" closer to the receiver.

"Oh, don't worry," I said. "She's okay."

"When'd this happen?"

"Last night. About two A.M."

"Shit, she left 'bout that time. Never came back."

"Yeah, she hooked up with me," I said. "She left her bag here last night, clothes and papers. I wouldn't be bugging you 'cept there's also some *pills*, prescription stuff."

"Really?"

"And I got this Boston gig, and don't wanna leave without getting it to her. Know where she is?"

"Naw, sorry."

"Where's she live?"

"Nowhere now, been crashing here last couple."

"Man. Do you think I could leave her stuff with you?"

"Well, I don't—"

"Fine," the excited background voice said, like he'd been listening ear-to-ear.

"Great," I said. "I'm leaving midtown right now, I'll come to you. Where at?"

"Uhm . . ." voice number one said.

"There's a Japanese restaurant," voice two interceded, "on the corner of Third Ave and Eleventh. We'll be seated at the sushi bar in ten minutes, eating tekka maki."

The call ended abruptly, the unit switched off. What the hell was tekka maki?

I dismissed that problem and worked on another: the bag of Gloria's stuff I didn't have. I went to the cabinet under my sink where I stored plastic bags and fished out the loudest, brightest one I could find, a pink plastic shopping bag with white drawstrings. Anyone carrying it would be easy to shadow from a distance.

I filled it with old socks and two T-shirts, then I went to my medicine cabinet and took down a plastic vial of ampicillin with nine red capsules left inside. I peeled off its label and dropped the vial in the bag with the socks and shirts, then pulled the drawstrings tight until the opening puckered. I tied three square knots and tucked in the ends.

Leaving the building, I stopped to check my mail. I was expecting the fee from the recent Syracuse job as well as a long-overdue expense check from a paranoid dry cleaner over in Queens. No mail yet.

As I headed for East Eleventh Street, walking by the closed

storefront of the Chungs' vacant deli, a light breeze blew up and fluttered a sheet of paper stuck in the gate. I would've missed it otherwise; it hadn't been there before. I plucked it out, opened it.

On the page were four columns of tight Korean script, the delicate letters like tiny pictures. I couldn't read it, but I stepped inside the dim newsstand nearby and made a photocopy of the note just the same. Just a magpie for clues.

When I walked out again, the renewed glare off the sidewalk hit me like a faceful of bleach. My unshaded eyes teared out of focus. I quickly put my sunglasses back on and the world became much clearer through their lenses of hunter green.

I put the note's original back in the gate where I found it. I lit and smoked a cigarette on the way to the sushi bar, which was on the southwest corner of Eleventh and Third. The three-story building was formerly an old pawnshop specializing in musical instruments (once a great meeting place for jonesin' rock musicians on the skids). It had been renovated and was now fronted with a bamboo pagoda façade, the slats shellacked a runny yellow-brown like nicotine-stained horse teeth.

Before I entered, I stopped to check the display menu. Tekka maki was tuna roll.

Inside, white-pebble gardens of toy shrubbery, mock waterfalls, and smooth pieces of driftwood reaching up out of the gravel like beseeching arms. The bleached hardwood floors gleamed like a layer of evenly spread honey.

To the right were tables, mostly occupied by couples, except for one long table in the back that hosted six businessmen in light shiny suits. To the left was the sushi bar in yellow pine and burnished steel, lit up like an operating theater. The air was odorless, absent any flavor. Behind a low glass shield, three men in immaculate kitchen whites carved up octopus and eel on white marble slabs, then molded the slices in with mounds of white rice, wrapping each one round with parchment-dry strips of scum-green seaweed. Uh . . . yum.

There were only two young men—late teens or early twenties—seated at the bar, so it didn't matter what they were eating. And my precaution of choosing a bright bag to shadow them by was also unnecessary. These two would've stuck out among mummers.

CHAPTER 6

The one closest to the door, at the far end of the bar, wore white-rimmed Foster Grant sunglasses too small for his head, pinching his temples. A long slender body and narrow waist, his midriff exposed in a clinging, yellow-and-black-striped top that made him look like a wasp (lowercase). His bare forearms were stringy, but his biceps well toned. Green golf slacks and black Frankenstein shoes completed his outré outfit.

His fine hair was hennaed the rich orange of candied yams and cut in a mod mop-top, but his eyebrows and chin stubble were jet black. Around his neck he wore a silver chain bearing an amulet of five outdated backstage passes—laminates—with ALL ACCESS printed across.

His friend, less flashy and alert, was striking in

his own way. At the moment concentrating on steadying the chop-sticks over his plate. His bleached-blonde hair was matted to his head and raked to one side like straw weed. From under it, I could only make out a snouty leprechaun nose.

He was wearing a plain white T-shirt, blue parachute pants, and souped-up Nike sneakers customized with six extra layers of plat-form soles tapered like pedestals.

The two men's odd appearance didn't faze me. In my experi-ence, the people who wear their complexities on the outside are much easier to figure than those who hide them deep within. *They're* the ones to watch out for. I was a practical example.

I took a breath, then swooped in on them, gushing, "Hello there, hello, thanks for meeting me on such short notice, out of the blue like this."

As the first one turned to look I was already sailing past him, taking the empty chair next to his friend. I surprised him when I sat down—approaching from his hair-blind side—and he jumped a little, but didn't look up from his chopsticks.

Without turning to either, I got a waiter's attention and ordered a Sapporo. Act normally, as if you're doing what you always do, and people usually take you in stride.

Henna-hair-and-white-sunglasses leaned forward and spoke across the other's brow.

"Payton?"

"Yeah, hi. Sorry, didn't get your name on the phone."

"I'm Seth," he said, his accent faintly continental. "This is Droopy."

"Droopy?"

"Yes." Seth offered no other explanation. None was needed. Droopy was swaying slightly in place, his upper body rotating in small counterclockwise circles.

I offered my right hand across for them to shake. Droopy shied away from it, but Seth countered by extending his left hand instead. Some lefties do that, make a point of letting you know it isn't exclusively a right-handed world. Which it isn't.

I didn't mind. I switched.

His grip was firm and dry, his fingernails smooth and conical. He had a small discreet tattoo on the web of skin between his forefinger and thumb: a little white daisy, five petals with a short green stem. No other body art I could see. His ears were pierced in several places, but most of the holes were empty, one silver stud in each lobe.

He tugged his white sunglasses low down his nose and peered at me, his plain brown eyes almond shaped.

"What happened to your poor face?" he asked, his concern genuine. "It's *awful.*"

Droopy turned to see for himself, parting his mesh of straw-colored hair.

"Brutal," he appraised.

Not that he looked all that good himself. Signs of excess, premature dissipation of youth, bags under his eyes the same color and texture of the raw tuna on his plate. Crust on his eyelids and sleep flakes on his long, long lashes. His eyes were the flat and colorless gray of paintbrush water.

I told them, "I was with Glo last night when she was attacked."

"Omigod, is she all right?"

"Yeah, she got away." I pointed to my face. "I preoccupied them."

Seth's index finger pushed his sunglasses back up his nose and applied pressure until his head was upright, too. He arched his shoulders back and shuddered.

"It hurts me just to look at you," he said.

"It hurts to be seen."

Droopy laughed, but too long after the remark. It might've been at some joke of his own.

My beer arrived in a tall silver mortar shell. I told the waiter no glass, but he left one anyway. I took a cold swig from the can of tart Sapporo, and said, "Ahh."

Rousing from a brown study, Seth said, almost to himself, "You forget how dangerous the city can be. You go along without any of the nastiness touching your life for so long, you start to disbelieve the stories you hear and read about rape and robbery. Then it jumps out at you from nowhere."

I sipped some more of my beer and nodded, smacking foam from my lips. "Except this came from somewhere. Those guys last night knew Glo. Said she had something didn't belong to her."

Seth put down his chopsticks, laid them in a neat right-angle cross on his plate.

"What?"

"I said, they said she had something of theirs."

Seth smiled thinly. "What? Did they say?"

"Not to me. I was wondering if you knew."

Seth shook his head. Droopy responded, too, wagging his scraggly bangs.

"Then maybe you know these three guys after her." I described the three.

Seth dabbed at the corners of his mouth with a linen napkin, clearing away a bright-green smudge of wasabi. "Sounds like a lot of people you see around."

"Where do you know her from?" I asked. "School?"

Droopy spoke thick-tongued, his breath rustling his long forelock like palm fronds. "Naw, she's jussa kid. Know err from the clubs."

"How long have you known her?"

"Not long," Seth answered for both. "New faces come and go. We started noticing her around . . . like, February. Danced with her a few times, but never really talked to her. The other night though, she needed a place to stay."

"When was this? Where?"

"Oh, who knows. Wednesday, I think, at one of the clubs. We never know where we are half the time anyway. But that doesn't prevent you from running into everyone—even if you'd rather *not*. Big as the city is, its strands converge like a spiderweb."

He smiled at his metaphor.

"Isn't Glo a little young to get into the clubs? I thought you had to be over twenty-one."

From Seth's vaulted expression, I guessed I'd inadvertently lapsed into speaking the dead tongue of ancient Aramaic. Hate when I do that.

His contempt rose frothily. "The clubs wouldn't *exist* without an underage clientele. They've got to let them in—or else there'd be nothing to be let *in* on. You get me? The clubs and the promoters know it. They give out the free passes."

"Like those." I pointed to the laminates displayed around his neck.

"What? Oh." He looked down, as if he'd forgotten he was wearing them. "Oh, well, *something* like these, but these are special." He petted one.

"And do they let in everyone, or only the exotic and the beautiful?"

Seth dismissed it with a swirl of his hand, the sorcerer unstirring a pesky spell.

"Beauty is in the eye of the bestower," he proclaimed. "If you truly *believe* you're beautiful, then others will believe, too. It's like the emperor's new clothes."

"Didn't he turn out to be naked?" I asked.

"Maybe, but for a while he had everybody saying how nice the fabric was. If you can get others to believe who you are, you are that," Seth said.

He was right. Up to a point. Attitude can always get you in the door, but once there, you have to deliver. But who was I to burst his bubble?

He continued unabated. "Take Droopy. He's a clothing designer. I keep telling him he's got to brag, to boast about himself. The only thing separating him right now from a *real* designer is making other people believe it. He made the shoes he's wearing. Show him your kicks, Droopy."

I looked down and checked out the multilayer platform sneakers. Each of the inch-thick layers of foam rubber was a different color: red, blue, yellow, green, orange, black, and purple.

"How do you keep them all together?" I asked. "Glue?" Droopy said, "Um, yeah, and staples and um—"

"Uht!" Seth said. "Trade secret."

I looked closer at the shoes. On the outside of the left insole, a small piece of metal stuck out that looked immediately familiar. It was the tab of a zipper, the teeth camouflaged by the heavy-duty staples attaching two of the layers.

I pointed. "Hey, that's cool. Is it to keep money in?"

He drew his feet in and tucked them under his chair, but the platform sneakers didn't quite fit and wedged there. For a second, he was stuck. Alarmed and bewildered, not knowing how to get out, he bounced up a few times attempting to stand, but finally cleared himself only by tilting far back in his chair, almost toppling over.

I reached out a hand and steadied him.

He grinned at me, his loose lips rubbery, a red sore in one parched corner. Then his face changed shades, blanching to ash white.

He said, "Skews," and scraped back his chair, springing off in the direction of the men's room. He moved nimbly on his pillared shoes, like walking on wedding cakes.

I turned to Seth. He made no comment, except to launch back into declaration.

"What was I saying . . . ? Oh, doesn't matter—what you have to understand about crusties, Payton, these nomadic roamers like Glo, is they're down here living on the streets for lots of different reasons. Some of them are slumming rich kids only *playing* homeless. Others are fugitives from their families, running from abuse. But all of them are hiding out in the city, living undercover here like mushrooms."

It was a little grueling and galling being lectured to about my city by some NYU undergrad, but then again maybe I needed to get back in touch.

"Living on what?" I asked.

"Whatever comes to hand. We live today in such a disposable society, all the means of survival can be found in the nearest garbage can: unwanted food and clothes, half-smoked cigarettes, magazines, and things to barter for whatever else is needed."

"But how 'bout when she needs cash in a hurry? Like when her dog was hurt?"

"Dog. She has a dog?"

"Uh, thinking of someone else. But still, cash in an emergency, say?"

"I don't know; steal CDs and resell them at the used shops, beg change from the tourists on St. Mark's Place, or sell sex. You know, chores. Whatever it takes."

"She said something about a job," I said, trying to make a connection. "She was *sitting* for someone in Brooklyn."

"You must mean Pow, the redheaded Berliner. He's an artist. She picks up extra cash modeling for him sometimes."

I laughed, then had to explain that I'd thought she'd meant she was *baby*-sitting.

Seth smirked. "Can you imagine? Her with a kid? But what was I saying? Oh, right—just that lately it's become like a trend to be homeless in the clubs. The clubs need the kids. They're both about discovery and reinvention. Teens finally finding a haven, to feel part of a community, a spontaneous environment of freedom where they can explore who they are—straight, gay, weird, whatever."

I got the feeling we'd veered off Gloria, and that maybe he was projecting a little of himself. I tried steering.

"What's Glo, in your opinion?"

"Well, you only have to look at her," he said. "She's butch as Tom Cruise."

"But she has a boyfriend—had, sorry. This guy Ted she was living with."

"Maybe, but look what she picked. A bruiser who'd smack her whenever she got out of line, a nobody who would drag her down to his nothing. Almost like she was punishing herself for her hidden desires, you know?"

"Hmmm, sorry, don't; I haven't met Ted, what's he like?"

Seth shrugged and laid his hands in his lap, gripping his thumbs in loose fists. "Me neither, well, never talked to him much whenever I saw them together. But then the clubs aren't conducive to conversation. Simply basic your-place-or-mine lines."

"What did you mean before, 'whenever she got out of line'?"

"Exactly that. She told me the other night, Ted thought because he'd picked her up off the street and took her in, she was his property. Weird shit, like who she could dance with. That's what finally wised her. I wasn't there, but Monday at some overcomped premiere at the Tunnel, she's dancing with some guy—not even straight, mind you—but Ted sees it from across the room and goes berserk. He runs over to them—doesn't even *look* at the *guy*—just backhands Glo into a column of speakers. And then—"

A high-pitched tone trilled twice, then twice more.

"Excuse me," Seth said. He reached into his hip pocket and removed a small black square. I thought it was his billfold until he flipped it open like a *Star Trek* communicator, which it was, in a way—his digital phone.

He said hello into it, then listened a while, and said, "God, I *know*. That's what I said. Once it stops charging, it wheels round and *gores* you. You should see Droop this morn. Haw!"

At that moment, Droopy returned from the men's room, looking riper. His platform step was springier. His eyes were brighter, more alert. There were light stains down the front of his T-shirt that hadn't been there before. Probably water he'd splashed on, except that his hair hanging down over his face was dry.

Before he sat down again, he flung back his head and flipped aside his hair, briefly exposing an elaborate tattoo on his neck. From below his right earlobe to the tip of his breastbone was a beautifully rendered Sacred Heart in vivid inks of red, orange, and purple, with green brier thorns pricking the bleeding tissue. I marveled at the workmanship; the inks alone had cost a small fortune.

Without pretense, I complimented him. "Excellent tattoo."

"Thanks," he said, and exhaled a cloying sweet chemical odor in my face. His smile was beatific. "Seth bought it for me. It was the most expensive one."

When he picked up his chopsticks again, Droopy's hands were surgeon steady.

Seth finished his call and refolded his phone to his pocket.

Droopy asked, "Who was that?"

"Natty," Seth said. "She wants to look over your drawings later."

"But I was going to—"

"*Droopy,* she's an important model, you need to—"

"Yeah, but . . ."

"No yeah-buts today."

I made getting-up-to-go noises, and drank the rest of my beer in two swallows.

"Well, I've really got to go," I said. "Oh—here's the bag. Thanks. It's been interesting talking to you both. I appreciate the insight."

Seth smiled sadly. "All bullshit, really. So, are you taking the train to Boston?"

Boston?

"Aw, no, the bus. Train's always late."

"Amtrak? Tell me! I always rent a car when I travel up to see my family."

The waiter came with the bill. Nine dollars! Reluctantly, I pulled out my wallet, but Seth snatched the check away.

"This one's on me," he said. "After your travail. Stop it! After what you've been through?"

"Well, thanks," I said, putting away my wallet unopened. Just the way it liked it.

"Don't mention it," he said, then a beat, "to *anyone.*"

I reached out to shake his hand, remembering to extend my left. Seth beamed warmly at me, grasping it, and shaking firmly as if I was the only one who truly understood.

To Droopy I just smiled, nodded. Then I left.

Nice kids all in all. I waited outside to see where they went next.

I found cover around the corner behind the restaurant's Dumpster, its rusted bottom leaking a slow drip of black filth into a tar puddle at my feet. An invisible steam of rancid fishslop hung heavy in the air.

I thought about what Seth had said, about coming to the city to make your dreams come true. When I was a kid, I wanted to grow up and be a Forties black-and-white private eye. And there I was, living my fantasy in Manhattan, hiding behind hot garbage. Too much color for my tastes—I lit up a cigarette to cut through it. Luckily, I didn't have long to wait.

Nor far to follow. From the restaurant, the two guys jaywalked across Third Avenue straight in front of a cab, jerking it—horn blasting—to a stop. Unperturbed, they went on to the corner, and into the chiseled-stone entrance of the NYU dorm.

Out front people were still loading up cars. I grabbed an empty milk crate off the sidewalk and followed the kids in as far as the lobby.

There was a desk presided over by two security guards, and a turnstile to pass through to get in. A sign over the desk read: ALL GUESTS MUST SIGN IN. Seth flashed the guards his school ID. Droopy stopped and signed in on a clipboard on the counter. Then they each passed through the turnstile and were gone from view.

Maybe they *were* students. Or at least one was.

For all I knew, Gloria might've been up in their room. But it wasn't likely, not when the three stooges knew it as a watering hole.

I walked away with some answers though. I took out the fax sheet from Matt and scribbled next to the digital phone's number: *Seth & Droopy—NYU dorm.* Where Gloria had come from the night before, before our lives entangled. I still had to figure out where she'd ended up. She had been going east. Ted Wylie's apartment was in that direction, and so was the café on Tenth and Avenue A. My stomach rumbled and reminded me I could eat something, too.

So I walked east.

As I walked down the sidewalk of Avenue A, I trod on a diamond-plate steel cellar hatchway. One hinge was broken and it sagged low beneath my weight, reminding me—like I needed it—not to trust the ground beneath my feet.

I stopped over at the café first. It was directly across from Tompkins Square Park, and located between a Laundromat and a retro-Seventies antique shop. In front, a short and stocky black-haired man in kitchen whites was hosing down the pavement. He looked Venezuelan, with dark, bluntly chiseled features.

Over the door, cemented into the arch, were letters in mosaic—bits of broken crockery, marbles, and mirror shards—spelling out: DOT.CALM.CAFE.

Inside it was a furnished cave lit by table lamps and ruby glass
ceiling fixtures. All the seats were torn and sagging, all random,
mismatched armchairs and sofas and vinyl kitchen chairs clus-
tered around two Formica tables.

Dark computer monitors sat in each corner of the room and
two were on the bar, where a young woman stood scooping coffee
grounds and shoveling them into a filter. There was a white phone
beside her. I looked around for the pay phone and spotted it back
by the rest room doors.

No one else was inside. I asked the woman if they were even
open yet. She blinked at me a few times, then—borderline aggra-
vated—said, "Brewing the pots."

"I'll wait."

I flipped through *The Weekly Cause*, one of the free papers
stacked on the floor. The Angry Letter from the Editor, Declan
Poole, accused the city of a secret policy of misclassifying violent
crimes against the homeless: ". . . to pad the recent record-low
crime rate, and increase the city's appeal to outside money—as
well as further His Honor's political ambitions—the city's homeless now die exclusively of 'natural causes.' Logic being: It's dangerous living on the street, so what's more 'natural' than they
should lose their lives?"

The coffee made, I got a large dark blend and a blueberry muffin. I sat down in a chair by the barred front windows, sipping my
coffee and eating pinches of muffin. It was good to have some
food in me. My perspective mellowed some and things began to
seem less bleak. My desperation grew quiet again.

I lit up a cigarette and gazed out at the high canopy of green
leaves over the park. Three chunky schoolgirls giggled by in
untucked white shirts and pleated, sky-blue culottes. Moving in
the other direction, a bald black woman pushed a stack of am-
plifiers on a dolly, its castors grinding grit. A heavy-faced old
man, with steel stubble and yellow-white hair, shambled by

complaining to himself in Russian, bits of foam forming on his cracked lips. I finished my coffee and wiped my mouth with a napkin.

I went across the street to Tompkins Square Park. The park was closed during the night and reopened at six A.M., when the dead-tired kids and the bums came looking for a soft patch of earth to lay a sheet of plastic or a bedroll on, and finally catch some Zs.

I walked around the favorite spots—under the trees, sheltered from the sun—and looked over every lump, looking for a lump like Gloria's. No such luck. The sleepers' drab clothes and hunched figures made identification impossible. For all I knew, she *was* there, hiding in plain sight amid her society of mushrooms.

Theodore "Teddy" Wylie's address was only a few blocks north and east. He hadn't answered when I called, but maybe he wasn't answering his phone. Supposedly Gloria was on the outs with him, but maybe that'd changed overnight now that she was in trouble. Only one way I could think of to find out.

I walked up Avenue A, then cut east on Eleventh. The street numbers were in the 500s. Another block to go.

Along the way, I stopped at several buildings where I saw stacks of take-out menus and flyers in the entryway or on the stoop. I collected them by the handful, a variety of throwaways advertising free delivery of pizza, burritos, curry, and chow mein. By the time I reached the end of the block, I had an instant disguise, now a guy there to drop them off.

I crossed Avenue B, and began stopping at every door on the odd side of the street and leaving behind menus as I worked toward number 617, a precaution in case anyone was looking. And in New York City, someone always is. Sitting at their windows looking out: the aged, the bored, the ill, and the clinically introverted peeking from behind drawn blinds. You never know when you're being watched. Hell, my bread and butter is observing people without their knowing it, so I can be excused.

The building at 617 seemed to tilt out above the sidewalk, its tin roof-façade sticking up like a pompadour, crusty with peeling brown paint. A five-story brick building, a story higher than those on either side. At several windows hung unpainted flower boxes growing only dry yellow stalks.

I opened the gate, its spring twanging eerily, and climbed the steps to the glass-and-metal door, jumping a little when the gate crashed closed behind me.

I ran my hand over the panel of numbered buzzers as if trying to find the right one, but I didn't push any, least of all T. WYLIE, #9. The old dodge of getting into a building by ringing all the bells is good for the movies—and even works in real life, too. The problem is all the sleeping dogs you wake (literal and not), and the darkened peepholes you have to pass on the way in. I didn't ring anyone, just seemed to, resting my hand on the door handle as if I were waiting to be buzzed in. Through the wire-mesh-reinforced glass, I saw no one in the entryway or stairwell.

I planted my right heel about an inch from the door, then stepped down, pushing my shoe up against it, bending back the toe. It wedged a crack about a quarter inch wide at the bottom. The latch strained against its socket. I took a deep breath, then coughed and hit the metal door frame hard and fast with my shoulder. The latch bolt popped out, the door swung open. Just the way the real take-out-menu guys do it.

The lock clicked shut behind me none the worse for wear. Not so my shoulder.

It was cooler and darker inside. The warped linoleum floor littered with cigarettes, junk mail, and a shriveled mouse on a gluetrap. A TV filtered through a door—muffled sounds of an afternoon talk show blaring the jeers of a studio audience sitting in abject judgment.

I started up the stairs, the steps springing disconcertingly. There were spots worn away like the holes in old shoes. I grabbed the loose bracketed handrail; it was like shaking a cane in the air.

The upper landings' lights were out. I pocketed my shades and read the door numbers by the silvery glow from the skylight four floors above. In the gloom, the tilt of the floor was exaggerated and for balance I groped my hand along the wall, its scaly surface dotted with old chewed gum.

Someone was simmering chicken in onions.

Apartment nine was on the fourth floor, rear, the only door at the end of the hall. Approaching it, I left behind what little light there was. To adjust, I closed my eyes and walked a few steps blind. My foot kicked an empty bottle and sent it spinning across the floor. It ended with a *chunk* against the door.

My eyes opened and I saw a pinpoint of light directly ahead. The apartment's peephole. I watched for the dot to go out as someone came to the door. It didn't. No one looked out, or passed in front of the light.

I moved forward invisibly until my outstretched hand found the door's surface. My knuckles rapped twice. Still no movement inside. My eye up to the peephole, I made out a tiny, upside-down and concave image of what lay beyond. The light was from an uncurtained window. I knocked harder, rattled the knob.

And the door cracked open, a sliver of daylight shooting out into the hall.

An overpowering odor leaked out. Instinctively, I shut my nose and mouth against it, but it built up instantly at the back of my throat as a noxious aftertaste.

I opened the door wider with my foot and the smell oozed out and bathed my face in a thick, sour wave, warmly worming into my hair, soaking through my clothes and onto my skin, my pores tasting it. My throat contracted trying to bar it from my lungs, but it was already in me. I gagged and savored its corruption more profoundly. It was the smell of decay that attracts dogs in the wild—and other animals whose nature it is to dig up old kills. I stepped in and closed the door behind me.

I had to get out of there. But I'd only just arrived.

I turned and locked the door for privacy. I had my choice of two dead bolts, a bolt below the doorknob, and a bar that fit into slots on either side, like a prison cell lockup. Tucking my hand into my sleeve, I locked one of the dead bolts.

I breathed through my teeth, but it didn't help. The trick is not to focus on the fact you're breathing the gases of rotting skin and human meat.

My stomach contents made a break for it, but I squelched the uprising. Icy sweat welled up in fat pimples on my back. I really had to get out of there. Soon.

The apartment was a one-room studio. I was in the kitchenette, next to the stove and a sink full of plates. I opened the cabinet underneath and found a near-empty bottle of Windex, unscrewed the nozzle, and poured its contents over my sleeve. The ammonia helped cut the awful air. I entered the room, my arm across my face like Bela Lugosi.

On the floor, the opposite side of a square kitchen table covered in coffee cups and newspapers, lay the toes-up body of a barefooted man. He was dressed in blue jeans and T-shirt, and had something like a half-inflated orange beach ball completely covering his head and neck. I moved closer, propelled by weird fascination.

It was a red and orange plastic bag from Tower Records, secured about his throat by a thin black electrical cord tied in three square knots. The plug was a solid black cube, an AC adapter wall wart, draped over his left shoulder. The other end's prong was over his right shoulder. I concentrated on the knots as a way to avoid seeing the body, untying them in my mind. The head was backed up to a chair, so whoever had tied the cord had straddled the man's chest. The knots were tied the way I would've tied them, right-handed.

The bag had suffocated him, plastic forming a vacuum seal

around his nose and mouth and eyes. But ineluctable time had passed. Bacteria, dissolving his tissue, had inflated the bag to the limp shape of a jack-o'-lantern in mid-July. The left side was caved in, stuck with something like tar to the hair and raw scalp on the inside.

Bile erupted in me—I couldn't see a bathroom door, but the one window in the room was straight ahead. I hopped over the body, rushing to get at it. My fingers feeling for the latch—already undone—I threw it open and stuck my head out. But the window didn't stay, it came rushing back down on me like a guillotine blade. I forgot being sick.

Recovering, I held the window open with my bare hands and took a wonderful gulp of unfetid outside air. I let the cool metal frame soothe down the back of my neck as I faced out over a courtyard overrun by weeds and rusted appliances. Across it stood another apartment building, every rear window bricked up by cinder blocks.

I looked around the room for something to prop the window open with. I saw, at the dead man's black-heeled bare feet, a two-foot-long chunk of pine two-by-four that looked cut just for that purpose. I walked over, but stopped short of picking it up. Flakes of dark dried blood were on one edge.

Panic rushed me back to the window, started me wiping it with my Windex-damp sleeve, even places I hadn't touched. Destroying evidence while creating new evidence of my very own, like a rank amateur. I forced myself to calm down, to stop, to look around, to see.

The custard-yellow walls were stark naked. A dusty sixty-watt bulb and a smoke detector hung from the cracked plaster ceiling concentrically ringed by brown water stains.

The body was on a tattered oriental. A thin black stain trailed from it, across the uneven floorboards to a corner of the room where a turned-over Coke can sat glued in its own syrup. A

brown-black cola stain was also down the front of the man's
T-shirt. The swollen flesh of his love handles peeked out eggplant
purple against the floorboards. A metal chain was attached to a
belt loop, linking up with a ring of keys in his right front pocket.
His wallet was crammed in his right rear, but I couldn't get at it
without moving him.

Five feet eight or nine. Mid-twenties or early thirties—hard to
judge without taking the bag off his head and I was *not* taking the
bag off his head. Heavyset and beefy, but that could've been the
gases bloating him.

On his right arm, from wrist to elbow, every inch of skin was
covered in a sleeve of tattoos, an intricate jigsaw puzzle design of
interlocking lizards sharing mutual tongues and tails.

Around his left forearm was a gauze bandage held in place by
white cloth tape. A small, sharp cut on the back of his hand where
the bandage ended had a familiar jagged shape. A toothmark, but
not human.

I reached down and pinched a corner of the tape with my fingernails and peeled it back, taking some dark hair away with the bandage. The arm rose freely—no more rigor mortis—and I had to
hold him down with my foot.

Lifting the bandage unleashed a vapor of decay. I had to squint
against it. A line of deep rips in the flesh, bleeding milky pink
pus, was unmistakably teeth marks, a dog's, and recent. I almost
recognized the smile. It had ripped through another intricate pattern of tattooed lizards on the left forearm. I reapplied the tape.

The rest of the room was two squat green-and-gold upholstered
armchairs set before a small round coffee table piled with cheese-
burger wrappers, dirty glasses, and two overflowing ashtrays. All
the filters were the same, Marlboro, and mixed in were several fat,
greasy marijuana roaches. Some of that might've settled my
stomach just then, but I was in enough trouble already.

The bed was a mattress on the floor, five lumpy pillows in

dingy vanilla pillowcases and wilted, flower-patterned sheets. At the foot were a stereo and a CD player, both switched on, their green readouts glowing silently.

Closer to the body was a plain walnut desk with two bottom drawers missing. The telephone was on top. The thing to do now was call the police and report it.

And when they asked me why I was there in the first place, I'd say . . .

What would I say? "Looking for the young woman who stole my watch."

Fine, sir. No need to talk to you further, sir. Have a nice day, sir.

Nuh-uh. They'd want it backwards, in triplicate, spelled *foh-net-ick-lee*, and I wasn't sure enough of my own innocent involvement to contrive answers that would convince trained skeptics. I did not call the police.

Next to the phone was an answering machine, its electrical cord missing. I lifted its lid; the spindles where a cassette should have been were empty. Negative space.

Using a pen, I opened the top drawer of the desk. It was crammed with canceled checks, ATM receipts, and overdue credit card bills—not that that made him a bad person in my book. Pay stubs made out to Ted Wylie (position: STAFF) gave me his Social Security number (the first three numbers 643) and the name of his last employer. Average take-home had been $225 a week. I took one of the stubs and the most recent phone bill and stuffed them in a pocket.

I looked in other drawers and found: curled photos of unknown people in sunny, sandy environs; matchbooks; loose AA batteries; a camera; a collection of lighters; and a selection of drugs—a plastic baggie of skunk-smelly red-threaded pot, a pellet capsule containing off-white crystals, and three yellow micro-mini zipper-lock bags as big as a baby's first tooth, full of white powder and imprinted with a tiny blue emblem of a rhinoceros horn.

Robbery as a motive was looking thin.

I picked up the camera, a heavy old Minolta with a chipped lens. Nine exposures advanced, if any film inside. Working under my sweatshirt, I pushed the release and rewound the crank, feeling something take. I opened the back and popped out a roll of film, ASA 1000, twenty-four exposures, and put it in my pocket.

I had to leave now. Nothing really rushing me but the corpse's inexhaustible patience.

I went to the door, checked out the peephole. An empty patch of lighted banister and dark shadows all around. I unlocked the dead bolt, using its knob to pull the door open a crack, then turned for one last look.

He was just some faceless guy, a few years younger than me, dead in his bare feet with a ridiculous bag over his head. Most likely it was Ted Wylie, but still a stranger to me. I felt undiminished by his death. But before I left I made a sign of the cross— nervously crossing the T twice—on the off-chance the gesture had mattered to him once.

Meeting no one going out or down the gloomy stairs was like winning Lotto.

I needed a cigarette. Quite possibly two or three smoked in hypersuccession.

When I got out the front door, I looked up and down the street. Two grizzled Latino men were drinking golden beer from a quart bottle on a front stoop two doors down. I headed away from them, farther east. I don't know if they paid any attention to me, but at the next few buildings I came to, I dropped off the rest of my take-out menus.

At the corner of Avenue D, I lit up a cigarette, sucking back the match sulfur along with the smoke of burning tobacco, scouring at the awful stench in my lungs.

I walked north up Avenue D as fast as I could without actually looking it. At Fourteenth Street, I caught a cab coming off the FDR and had the driver take me home. He didn't mind my smoking in his cab; he was smoking himself, a cigar. I'm not an aficionado, but it smelled excellent, more fragrant than the freshest flower.

And the distance we put behind us was softer than a featherbed.

CHAPTER 8

No new messages on my answering machine. I stood still just inside the door and looked around my apartment. The squalor reminded me too much of the room just vacated. My underwear strewn on the floor, shirts, jeans, and dirty socks kicked into one corner. Spilled-over stacks of magazines slated for recycling.

The air was stale, stagnant. I crossed the room and opened the windows to get a crosscurrent of warm air going, swirling in dust eddies.

Up on the mantel, over the twin radiators, were framed photos of my parents, my college friends' kids, Matt Chadinsky and his wife, Jeanne, at the agency's annual barbecue, Mrs. Chung behind the deli counter making me a roast beef sandwich, my attorney Marguerite Laubach in

Finland on a bobsled (her crazy black curls snaking out from under the baby-blue crash helmet). No pictures of Clair, or her art—my collection stored in a walk-in closet at my parents'—no immediate *textural* evidence that I was still carrying the torch.

And I wasn't, really, carrying it anymore. Having burned so long and far down, it had set my hand ablaze, the cold fire now a part of me; I couldn't drop it even if I wanted to.

If.

I started cleaning my apartment. There were three dirty glasses, four empty paper cups, and two full ashtrays on my coffee table. I stacked the cups and ashtrays, carried them into the kitchen, and dropped them on top of a full wastebasket. Clawing the glasses together in one hand, I carried them to the sink—already a mess of glassware, mugs, and silver. No cooking utensils or plates. I squirted in creamy dishwashing liquid and, with the water running, I began washing and rinsing.

Before I knew it, the sink was empty and clean glasses were drying on the rack. I sopped up the water on the counter and threw the paper towel away. I lifted the trashbag from the basket and tied it. I put in a fresh bag. Then I went around the apartment gathering up dirty clothes.

Cleaning was the sort of mindless activity I needed just then, my ideas always flowing more freely with my hands busy. I figured out some things. And on top of that, by two o'clock I had an apartment I wouldn't mind being found dead in.

The man's death meant nothing to me personally, and for all I knew he'd deserved it. But the girl was mixed up in it somehow and I was somehow mixed up with the girl (or simply mixed up). Either *way*, I needed to know as much as I could.

Plainly, he hadn't died accidentally, but it's always good routine to rule out the obvious. Nor had he committed suicide; everything else aside, a suicide would've locked his door.

Murder then. The who, the what, the where, I thought I knew. The when?

Rigor mortis had resolved itself and the man's muscles had gone flaccid. Dead over thirty hours. Or longer, depending on the weather the day before. I'd have to check, but tentatively late Wednesday or early Thursday morning. Any longer and I would not have been able to stand thirty seconds in there.

Something else to go by was the dog bite on his arm. He was the one who stabbed Pike with the beer bottle, probably to get him to let go. Gloria had taken the dog to the vet's Tuesday morning. The white gauze bandage on Wylie's arm was clean, no blood soaked through, so it hadn't been a first dressing. A second bandage had been applied after the bleeding stopped. All this at least gave me a framework to tack other facts onto, and ask further questions. Like, how? Like, why?

Robbery didn't seem a likely motive but I had no way of knowing what was missing, only what *wasn't*: his wallet, stereo, a camera, and a selection of drugs. It could've been an interrupted theft, but why would the perp stick around to apply the bag to the guy's head and leave behind the goods?

No indications of a premeditated attack. The hunk of wood he'd been struck with belonged in the apartment, same with the electrical cord, and maybe the plastic bag, too.

Suffocating him with the bag meant the blow to the head hadn't killed him, so whoever dealt it was a strong person checking his or her swing, or a weak one giving his or her all.

Not a random act; the missing answering machine cassette meant prior contact with the victim—at least one phone call. No signs of a struggle, a spontaneous attack. Supporting this was the soda can and the stain down his shirt, as if he'd been hit on the head while taking a sip, at his ease with someone he knew—thought he knew.

Nothing at all on the scene pointed to a hit, nothing remotely professional about it, amateur night all-round. And me emceeing. Hopefully that meant the cops would clear it all up without my ever having to get officially involved.

Just keep telling yourself that, I told myself.

I lit up and smoked.

The phone rang. I let the machine answer. It was my mom. I picked up.

She said, "Hi, dear. Didn't you get my messages?"

"Oh, just got back, Mom. Haven't had a chance." I made room on my desk and emptied my pockets. A phone bill, a pay stub, a roll of film. "How're you guys?"

"Thank you for my flowers," she said sweetly. "I have them here in front of me."

I smoothed out the phone bill, reading over Ted Wylie's long distance charges. They covered the period from March 27 to April 29. "I'm glad you like them," I said. "How's Dad?"

"He's out with the dogs. They're worse than kids."

Most were San Antonio, Texas, numbers, but in the last week of April three calls were made to Burlington, Vermont, all for under a minute. I kept things rolling with Mom. "Weather's been nice here."

"Beautiful here, too. We've been eating dinner outside on the patio every night."

"Sounds great."

I looked at the pay stub. In addition to Ted Wylie's SSN, it gave the name and address of his last employer, Ellis Dee Entertainment Productions, Inc., on West Twenty-first Street.

"Have you been eating, dear?"

"Yes, Mom. Thanks for asking."

"You've got to eat," she said seriously. "How's everything else? What have you been up to?"

"Oh, ya know . . ." I slid the papers aside. "All your worst fears coming true."

"Business better?"

I twirled the roll of film on my calendar blotter. "Well, business is business," I said.

"And . . . ?"

My mom had a preternatural ability to tell when something was wrong. I only wish she'd passed it on to me, but I guess actually it's a mother thing.

I heard a buzzing from the corner of my desk. Gloria's beeper vibrating again. I'd almost forgotten about it. I picked it up and read the number of the incoming call. It was the pay phone at the dot.calm.cafe.

"Mom, I got to go. I've got to call this person back."

"Who? A client?"

Being a snoop, on the other hand, I got from her.

"No, it's . . ." An idea surfaced: If I dialed the pay phone, I'd get only a faceless voice, no way to track the person it belonged to. Unless . . .

"Mom, got a pen? Now? Good, take this down." I read off the pay phone number. "Call that in fifteen minutes. Set the oven timer."

"Who is it?"

"Doesn't matter, hang up as soon as someone answers. Okay?"

"Is this something you're working on?"

"No, it's—look, just—I'm helping test a friend's phone, but I've got to be there to . . . Look, just call the number, okay, Mom?"

"Okay, okay, you don't have to shout."

"I'm not shouting," I said, then brought it down a notch. "Okay?"

"I love you."

"Love you too. Don't forget to make the call."

"You just make sure you eat."

"Yesssss. G'bye."

I had fifteen minutes to get back to the coffeehouse on Tenth and A. I used five of them to change my clothes. Just good routine, really, altering my general appearance before going over the same ground again, but also . . . the rot of death was still on me.

A pair of black jeans and a blue sweatshirt with a frayed collar.

I also changed my sunglasses to a pair of darker-tinted tortoise-shell Wayfarers.

I brought along the roll of 35mm film, and on the way dropped it off with my card at a one-hour-photo shop on Avenue A. I was back in business.

I got to the café with three minutes to spare.

Seven customers were inside, scattered around the cool, dark room. None of the computer monitors were on, all the keyboards and screens dusty; the fad there already fading. Maybe one morning everyone would wake up and notice, "Hey, we're not in outer space yet—we've only been *circling* and *circling* the planet. Still trapped here!"

Nobody was at the rear of the room back near the pay phone.

I ordered a large dark blend, which left me with three dollars.

The woman behind the counter gave me a puzzled look sliding my cup across.

"You changed your clothes," she said.

I smiled and shrugged.

In front of the cash register were piles of postcards advertising local nightclubs and concert appearances by bands like Bowery Angels and Lowdown Payment. I grabbed a handful of club in-vites and sat down in a cracked-vinyl chair by the door, pretending to read them while sizing up the customers.

A pasty-faced young couple with matching vermilion hair were fast asleep, slumped down on a long low settee, their slack, puffy faces breathing fitfully as foundry stokers. Another couple, more vertical at the other end, were speaking French and waving filterless cigarettes in the air, spinning out blue smoke and snipping off wisps.

A young man with curly brown hair wearing Walkman head-phones and sunglasses like old-fashioned welding goggles sat semisilently mouthing a song. Seated across from him, a young woman was writing in a rice-paper journal. A chicken-necked man with tarnished white hair and face stubble like embedded glass sat at the bar talking to the woman on duty while she steamed milk for his cappuccino.

Five minutes passed and the pay phone didn't ring; I started worrying Mom had forgotten, or called too soon. Served me right either way, using her as an operative.

Idly, I shuffled the postcards I'd gathered, reading over the invites to local clubs (distributed throughout the Village in the thousands):

Shake Your Weekend-Weary Booty after-hours at Fugitive's Den,
113 Orchard St. 1 blk. below Houston & west of Ludlow.
Doors open 4 AM—'Til?

Thursday Night Trip Hop in The Underbrush,
296 W. 14th St., resident DJs Marcus & Mike Sike.
Doors open 10:30 PM, $7 w/flyer.

One in particular caught my eye:

Ellis Dee Entertainment presents Raven Lunar Chic,
Every Friday Midnight at Hellhole, 66 W. 21st St.
Industrial, Gothic, and Dark Electronica in 9 rooms of feverish dancing.
Move your abused bodies to music mixed and manipulated
by master DJ St. Sane.

"Seek and ye shall find," I murmured, slipping the card in my back pocket.

Finally, the pay phone rang. I looked up to see who'd answer it, but no one in the room moved. Motion and light at the back. The rest room door swung open and a tall thin man stepped out and stopped the phone ringing. It was the man in denim with the black Fu Manchu I'd seen gardening in the vacant lot.

I was too far away to hear what he said, but suddenly he craned his neck back from the receiver, and looked startled. I waited for him to hang up. And waited.

He spoke into the phone, then listened, and then listened some more.

Not good. Hang up, Mom.

The man stiffened. He inclined his head within the receiver and cast a long probing look around the room. I kept my eyes in front of me, fumbling out a cigarette.

Maybe it wasn't her at all but someone else on the line.

I lit the cigarette, then dropped it in the ashtray after only one puff.

The man, holding the phone to his chest, raised his voice, deep and slightly sibilant like he had a tooth or two missing, and called out, "There a Payton here?"

Terrific. My choices were sit there and ignore him as he had a chat with Mom or get up and tip my hand—tip my hand completely. Not much choice; I had to find out what she'd told him. I got up and walked over, smiling.

He studied me from behind murky orange-lensed shades.

I said thanks and grabbed the receiver. He passed by without a word, emitting a warm odor of fertilizer.

"Hello," I said.

"Oh, hi, dear, good, I thought I'd dialed the wrong number. Your friend Jimmy didn't seem to know who—"

"Mom, you're killin' me here. What'd you say?"

"Say? Nothing."

"I told you just hang up."

"Oh, I know, but I forgot to mention—and you *never* return my calls—but Sally Marshack's daughter is going to be in the city this weekend looking at schools. I gave her your number. I knew you wouldn't mind showing her round. She's very attractive, and smart. She's going to be a marine biologist."

"That's great, Mom, but you're sorta ruining the moment here."

I looked around the café. The man was gone.

"Look, gotta go. Call ya later."

I rushed to the door and looked out, but couldn't see the denim man anywhere up or down the sidewalk. Then I glimpsed him across the street going into the park.

I left behind my undrunk coffee and a cigarette smoldering in the ashtray. Such waste, while in Third World countries drowsy smokers dozed off in sweatshops.

The Tenth Street entrance to the park was a large paved area where people were Roller-blading and playing hoops. Jimmy entered farther down on East Ninth, by the preschool swing sets and jungle gyms. I followed at a distance, keeping his denim hat in sight.

Inside, the three-block-wide park was an abundance of vibrant greens, a soothing eye relief from the prevailing gray stone and red brick of the city. To my left, a line of wooden benches, occupied by couples and men alone. Near the stone drinking fountain were two men in wheelchairs, one watching the pigeons and squirrels forage in the grass, the other spinning in circles and poppin' wheelies, balancing himself between the spoked wheels, rockin' the cradle.

Jimmy had a hoppity gait easy to keep track of from a safe distance; either he was hurrying or limping or both—maybe a bum leg.

Stepping out of the shade, I felt the afternoon sun come down on me hard.

A green pickup truck from the Department of Parks and Recreation was idling before a small squat brick building housing the only public rest rooms in the area. Here the path joined other paths curving through the park.

Jimmy kept going straight east.

Looking around, it was hard to believe that when I'd first moved to the East Village the park had been in severe disrepair, uncared for, and abandoned like many of the buildings around it. Buildings vacated during the Seventies by landlords unable to afford their upkeep were later invaded by heroin and crack dealers, who claimed them as strongholds and dens for addicts and prostitutes. Their presence drove out the regular folk, before strings of fires—accidents and arsons—forced nearly everyone out. The neighborhood became untenable.

During that time, Tompkins Square Park was taken over by the homeless. Hundreds, young and old, established a shantytown on its grounds, a diverse community of anarchists. Others claimed abandoned buildings nearby as squats and vacant lots as public gardens. The city took no notice until a real estate boom in the Eighties saw developers buying up cheap property east of A. Suddenly it was in the city's best interest to improve the park and make the neighborhood attractive to wealthy outsiders with the means to pay exorbitant rents *and* higher taxes. This was called progress.

In August 1988, the city tried to impose a curfew on the park to oust the homeless. Over four hundred policemen arrived in full riot gear, some mounted on horseback, some in low-hovering helicopters. A bottle was thrown from the crowd and a brutal neighborhoodwide riot erupted, lasting long into the night. Thereafter, the

park was closed off by high chain-link. A concrete band shell—
once a public performing space and popular shelter from the
elements—was demolished. Later, in redevelopment, the city
gave back a park for families to picnic in on Sundays, but it never
rebuilt the band shell. Nor found a place for the homeless, who
scattered themselves to other, smaller retreats.

Ahead on a bench, a black man in a mustard-brown T-shirt, his
slick muscular arms the color of bronze, called over to Jimmy,
"Hey-hey-hey, Mistuh Green-Jeans."

Jimmy stopped, looked, and went over grinning. They met in a
complicated handshake that ended with each stamping the other's
clasped hand with a fist. Jimmy looked in my direction, but not *at*
me leaning against the fence of the dog run watching a stippled
Great Dane prance around an Irish setter that was digging its front
paws into woodchips. What with the aroma of the cedar basking
in the sun, I could hardly smell the shit going down.

Out of the corner of my eye, I saw Jimmy on the move again,
walking toward the exit onto Avenue B (a.k.a. Charlie Parker
Place). I thought I knew where he was going, so I hung back a little. On either side of the lane were ancient oak trees, tall and
thick, stretching leafy boughs that arched high in the middle. The
ground pulsated with brush strokes of sunlight filtering down
through their swaying branches.

Birds chirping and squirrels chattering, newspaper skidding
across the pavement, kids grinding by on skateboards. Behind
me, soft tires crunched pebbles and an engine hummed. I turned
and saw a blue-and-white police cruiser creeping up.

The female officer riding shotgun gave me a long, blank look
as the prowl car went smoothly by and pulled out onto Avenue B
going south.

I couldn't see Jimmy anymore, but I wasn't worried, figuring
he was headed back to the garden lot where I first saw him. Still, I
crossed the street at a jog.

On the southeast corner was the rebuilt Trinity Lower East Side Lutheran Parish. Farther down, most of the buildings were deserted. Rusted gates locking entryways, steel shutters drawn down. Not even the graffiti were fresh. I read as I walked— SWOOP, CAPO, GIPSY, M$, L.E.S./RIP—when a dark shape rushed out at me from an alleycrack between two buildings.

I leaped back and collided flat against a soft solid form behind. I tried to turn but suddenly powerful brown arms descended on me tight as tongs, trapping my hands by my sides. I hadn't heard him coming up behind me; he'd been careful, I'd been careless.

Hauling me off my feet, he slammed me down again, hard against my heels, the impact jangling my organs inside and out. My sunglasses flew off. Pain resurrected throughout me, inducing a newborn anger.

I arched my shoulders and wrenched backward, smashing the top of my skull into his face. I was aiming for nose cartilage, but caught hard chin-edge instead, doing myself more harm than good, resoundingly ringing my chimes.

He lifted me again. This time I bent my knees to keep him from snapping a bone. I flopped down onto pavement, flat on my ass.

Jimmy leaned down into me, his bug-eyed, orange-lensed sunglasses close to my face. In their dull reflections, my head looked bigger than usual.

I didn't know what to say that wouldn't land me in more trouble than I was already in. Not that either Jimmy or his friend—the guy from the park bench—was taking cues from me. They grabbed me and dragged me into the narrow alley that reeked of urine and feces, my feet kicking glass and rusted bed frames.

We came out in the back courtyard of the buildings, the two upper floors caved-in, half-demolished by fire. No help then from gawking onlookers.

Then Jimmy's friend tossed me onto a mound of brick rubble. He held me down as Jimmy went through my pockets. He pulled

out the club invite, the photo receipt, my cigarettes, and something I hadn't realized I'd brought along: the fax sheets from
Matt, covered with my notations about Gloria/Glo.

He read the pages over then stuck them into a breast pocket of
his denim shirt and buttoned it.

Stepping in closer, he asked me, "Wire you looking for
Glory?"

I misunderstood, said, "What? I'm not."

A nod from Jimmy and his friend shook me hard and fast like
an industrial agitator mixing cans of oil-base. "Answer him," he
said, baring teeth, two metal.

"Gloria stole my watch last night."

They say the truth shall set you free, but it had no effect on them.

Jimmy fished out my wallet, his hands trembling like he had
the shakes; maybe he did. Glad I wasn't the only one nervous. He
flipped it open and read my license and ID. Not impressed. He
looked through the billfold, not touching my last few dollars but
pulling out the credit card receipt from the veterinary hospital.
He read it.

"What the—"

He read it again. Then took off his sunglasses and stared down
at me. His right eye was green with brown flecks, but his left eye
was covered over by a murky film like mother-of-pearl inlay.

He asked me, "You paid a hundred twenty dollars on my dog's
vet bill?"

"Pike's *your* dog?"

He smoothed down his Fu Manchu, then shot a glance to his
friend, and shook his head. "Ray, you can take off, man. Got this
covered."

Ray thought it over, deciding for himself. "Your problem's
mine, man. You sure?"

Jimmy nodded.

Ray let go of me and said, "Later." He left the way we came in.

I reached up my hand to Jimmy, and said, "My wallet."

"Some answers first. Who're you working for? Who's looking for Glory?"

"That's two separate questions," I said, getting to my feet. "First, I'm not working for anyone. Like I told you, she's got my watch; she took it last night after three guys got through stomping me. I'm just trying to get it back. As for your second question—it's a good one— I'd like the answer, too. For starters, the three who stomped me, maybe you know 'em, skinhead-types? One's named Stosh. He thinks your friend has something belongs to some guy named LSD."

As I heard myself say it, I made a connection I hadn't before. LSD. Ellis Dee. Ellis Dee Entertainment Productions. Ted Wylie's employer. Damn.

"Don't know them," Jimmy said, "but I've seen them, they were by my place yesterday sniffing around for Glory, just like you. The fucks, they're flipped if they think she stole their shit."

"Didn't she?"

"She didn't take a damn thing."

"Sure, sure, I buy that. Her stealing my watch and all, I can vouch for her character. Maybe that's the least of her problems now anyway. Still, it could go right to the top if I hand it all over to the cops. Only, nobody needs that kind of hassle, and all I really want is my watch."

Empty threat, me of all people waving cops.

He sucked in his cheeks, thinking, then blew them out again like he was blowing a smoke ring. He tossed me my wallet and cigarettes.

"Let's take a walk to my place," he said, then turned and started out.

"How come?" I asked.

"You want your watch, don't you? I've got it."

"*My* watch?"

"Gold Rolex, right?"

I followed between the two buildings in silence, tripping over the same rubble.

My sunglasses, like some giant squashed insect, lay broken out on the sidewalk. Someone, probably me, had stepped on them in the struggle. I stopped to light a cigarette. Catching up to Jimmy, I asked, "How'd you get my watch?"

"She came by this morning. Gave it to me to sell. To get my dog out of hock."

"Did she tell you what happened to Pike?"

He nodded, sour-faced.

"Did she tell you who did it?"

"Yep, Ted. That fucker."

But that's all he said. A very forgiving nature, I thought, too forgiving.

My silence on the subject made him nervous. His walk became a little more erratic, like he was concentrating too hard on keeping his stride normal, only normal's hard to fake, and plain alien under stress.

He said finally, "Ted got bad as he gave. Pike fucked him up good. Believe it! Glory went over there to get her stuff. She was finally moving out, but was afraid Ted would try to stop her. I said I'd go along, but she thought I'd make it harder. I made her bring Pike though. Pike worships her. Ted made the monumental mistake of grabbing Glory in front of him. Pike objected."

"Chomp."

"Exactly." He laughed, but that sounded unnatural, too; he was still holding back, concealing—the concealment more a revelation than what he was revealing.

"What did Ted say when you saw him?" I asked.

"What do you mean?"

"How'd he explain what he'd done to your dog?"

He shrugged. No explanation.

I asked, "How long you known Glory?"

"Met her in the park couple months ago. Got to having coffee. She'd come by and take Pike out. He loves to explore, but I can't with the leg. Steel plate in my knee." He struck it with a ringed finger, the two metals ringing even muffled by cloth and flesh.

"You two only friends or more than friends?" I asked.

"There's nothing *more* than friends, man."

"What I mean is, are you the reason she left Ted?"

"Hey, she's young enough to be my *grand*daughter. I only told her she had to get away from that prick. He slapped her 'round. She finally wised up on her own. I only offered her another option, a place to stay. She didn't take me up."

"I see."

He should've had a bigger grudge against Ted and didn't. As we walked along he told me he knew where Ted's place was. He even admitted going there the morning after Glory left and never returned with his dog. After Pike got cut up, she brought him straight to the vet's, and was too scared to go back to Jimmy's and tell him what had happened. She was afraid of his reaction, and didn't get up the courage for two days. For a day and a half then, Jimmy hadn't known what'd happened to either one of them.

I wondered if he would have admitted all that to me if he'd killed Ted. I didn't know. His story sounded thin either way, and maybe it was wiser to steer clear of the subject altogether on the off-chance he did.

When we got to his garden lot, he pulled from his pocket a braided nylon key ring with two keys on it. One unlocked the motorcycle-chain lock. He unstrung the chain and opened the gate wide till it slammed on the inside against a garden gnome, its empty face already pummeled into plaster dust. I followed him in, letting the gate swing shut, the loose chain rattling and clanging against the lead pipe.

Jimmy took hold of a hoe leaning against a gnarled crab apple tree in white blossom. Using the hoe as a staff, he walked up the path, past dark earth beds with yellow-blooming forsythia and and blueberry bushes sprouting early green. Along the east perimeter he had a vegetable garden of rhubarb, tomatoes, cucumbers, and stringy, purple-flowered chives.

Several sun-bleached, marrowless dog bones were strewn in the dirt around the yard. An old grocery cart was parked by a cluster of wild white daisies.

I asked how long the garden had been there.

"Four years. Cleared it out myself. There used to be two burnt-out Pintos here."

We walked to the far end of the lot, to the door of the toolshed. A large oil drum full of rainwater stood outside it, at its base a collection of labelless Clorox jugs.

The shed door was a wide woodplank that looked like just another panel of the patchwork wall except for a pair of hinges and a padlocked hasp. Jimmy inserted a key in the thick steel padlock and turned it, unhooked the padlock, and swung back the metal strap. Then he rehooked the padlock on its loop and pushed the door in with an audible crypt-creak. He held it open, ushering me in.

I hesitated. It was dark in there.

But I was trying to give the impression of playing it square, so I had to dumb-down my instincts. Not far to go but they still didn't like it one bit as I bent to clear the door's lintel and enter the inky confine.

I stayed a little crouched inside, afraid a roof nail would spike my scalp if I stood up straight.

Jimmy came in after and the door swung shut. I'd forgotten to close my eyes before entering, and from brightness of day I was left momentarily blind. I could hear movement around me, but couldn't see Jimmy until he blocked several pinpricks of light stealing through gaps in the boards. Slowly, as my eyes adjusted, I made out hundreds of these tiny holes, straining in the daylight as through a colander.

I took a step forward. The floor was soft like carpeting. I looked down: it was carpet. A wide remnant of burgundy medium shag, dark with soil stains, paw prints, and dirty boot marks. Another step, I kicked something dull that rolled a few inches. It was a thick, knotted rope, a dog's chew toy. Also on the ground were an empty water dish and a folded Navajo blanket covered in tawny bristles.

A small space, only nine feet by six. In one corner, a foam mattress and bedroll. No garden tools in sight. Not a toolshed at all, but Jimmy's home.

Milk crates were piled four high in four columns against the back wall, some storing dry foods, canned goods, and bottled water; others sweaters and socks; utensils, plates, and candles; and books, mostly paperbacks. I noticed well-thumbed copies of *Tom Brown's Field Guide to City and Suburban Survival* and *The Complete Poems of Emily Dickinson*, as well as several pamphlets and booklets published by Narcotics Anonymous. One crate had a bumper sticker: I ♥ N.A. & N.A. ♥ me.

Halfway into the room was a clumsy-looking machine with a tank attached to it. I bent down to look at it closer. A coiled heating panel on the front and the stink of kerosene. A kerosene heater, banned in New York City, this one practically an antique, but in well-oiled, working condition, and full of fuel. I guessed I wouldn't be smoking.

I jerked a thumb at it, asking, "Aren't these sorta dangerous?"

"So is hypothermia," Jimmy said, looking at me over his shoulder, not turning his body away from where he crouched by an open footlocker. I assumed he was getting my watch. He'd taken his sunglasses off and his bad eye was again visible, its milky retina pierced by a thread of daylight. I turned away.

He had a completely livable space there, all his basic needs met, even some meager comforts like a radio-cassette player and makeshift washbasin. And his kitchen was better stocked than mine would ever be.

I saw three well-used sketch pads on top of one of the crates. One was open to a pencil drawing of a dog, clearly Pike, signed by the artist: J.J. Not realistic in style—the form translated more as Alien—but nonetheless it captured the strength of the animal's muscles and his attitude of expression.

I turned to compliment Jimmy on it and forgot what I was going to say.

Something glinted in his right hand. Not my watch—longer and thinner. Shiny but not gold—a wickedly curved silver serrated edge.

A tardy thought occurred to me then: *If I really need a Rolex this badly, I can buy another.* Knowing the time was overrated anyway. In that musty shack, time faltered, slowing to a sluggish drip, clogged up by fear and anticipation.

My eyes held his knife as the tight focus of my universe.

Too bad he couldn't keep it steady. Bright prism flashes playing off its keen edge slashed back/forth, up/down, over and across my eyes.

A dry, wheezy whistle emanated from his throat as he stared at me, his mismatching eyes coldly concentrating on my face.

Perversely the old carpenter's rule came to mind: "Measure twice, *cut* once."

CHAPTER 10

have what I consider a healthy—if not awe-some—respect for sharp objects in other hands. It is a fear I never want to conquer, only temporarily to quell.

Blandly, I said, "So, you belong to N.A.?"

I got no answer except a flinch as if I'd directed a sudden move at him. He was strung-out, unpredictable. If he came at me, there was no place for me to go. The door opened *in*, and for all I knew he'd latched it behind us. A single step in any direction and I'd be cornered in the shack. Standing my ground in the center at least gave me room enough to duck to all sides, only one move in every direction, like a king in endgame.

I asked, "What were you addicted to?"

He still didn't speak, but also didn't attack.

Just held the knife shaking in his hand, bouncing incidental light all over my face. It was driving me clear to the edge of reason. I was going to do something stupid soon.

The closest thing to grab to defend myself was the kerosene heater, heavy enough to do some damage. I could throw it at him and use the extra second to open the door and get outside. Problem was, if full of fuel, the heater might've been *too* heavy.

"Look," I said, "I can take a hint, you want me to go, right?"

"Heroin," a dead voice answered. "Was my drug of choice. *Not* my addiction."

He tightened his grip on the knife, flexing ropy muscles in his long fingers. He concentrated his hand steady.

"We've got these voids, empty spaces," he said, "some of us— maybe all of us—inside us. You got to fill it with something. People try smoke, alcohol, God, violence . . . You smoke, right? So maybe you can understand a little. There's a poem goes, 'Water, is taught by thirst.' So true. My lesson was heroin."

"*Was* heroin?" I asked. "No more?"

"Always. What do you mean? Right now, I'm trying. Trying always. Monday I check into St. Vincent's program again. Another second chance . . ."

"A friend of mine kicked it," I said. "He belonged to N.A."

"What's his name, maybe I know him."

"Doubt it, but Mark. An English poet out of D.C."

"No, don't know him. How long's he been clean?"

"Well . . . he's dead now. The bug."

"Yeah. Yeah. I'm lucky so far. Sorry."

While on his good side, I asked, "Is Gloria using, too?"

Mistake.

He flared and raised the blade higher.

I leaned toward the heater, felt a muscle pull in my side. Terrific.

His good eye burned sharp and fierce.

"What? No way! She'd never touch it. Hates drugs. Her mom's a big cokehead living off a divorce settlement in Vermont. Glory'd never use. I'd never let her."

"So . . . she doesn't have that void you were talking about?"

"Hey, what do you think taking up with that asshole Ted was about? Her father booked on her and her mom when she was seven. She's still trying to fill that gap. And *that's* a hard nut, maybe harder to crack than the shit. But I couldn't tell you."

I said, "Hey, maybe it's none of my business"—and doubly so with you waving that knife around—"but it sorta sounds like you need to take in a meeting."

It made him mad, but something still held him in check.

He accused, "Did you really pay a hundred twenty dollars on my dog's vet bill?"

I didn't answer, he'd seen the receipt. Anyway, what he really wanted to know was why I'd do such a thing. I didn't have an answer for that either.

He tossed the knife in the air, end over end, and as it came down blade first, he gripped it by the handle and drove the knife into a bare patch of earth at his feet. He stood up straight and looked at me a long time, smoothing down his Fu Manchu with opposing forefinger and thumb.

"Pike means a lot to me," he said finally. "Survived last winter thanks to him. We were snowed in for three days and ran out of fuel for the heater. We kept each other alive."

He reached into the front pocket of his jeans and pulled out my gold Rolex. He'd had it with him all along.

"Here you go, man. Be careful with it. Try not to lose it again. The Village ain't the Village no more. It's the land of plenty of nothing."

I took the gold watch in my hand. It was mine all right, but heavier than I remembered it. The crystal face lightly scuffed, the raised bubble-window over the date scratched opaque, it had run down at eleven past nine that morning.

Jimmy walked to the shack door and opened it, daylight flooded in. He stooped to exit. I was right behind.

Outside, squinting against the wide expanse of sky—an unmitigated blue, not a shred of cloud disturbing—my confidence returned.

I said, "I need those papers back."

"What papers?" He looked at me like he didn't know what I was talking about.

I pointed to his shirt pocket, unbuttoned now. He tugged it open and showed me it empty, the papers gone. He must've put them in the footlocker when his back was turned to me.

"Guess you dropped them," he said. "What do you need them for now anyway? You got your watch."

"They're mine."

"You're too hung up on possessions, man. Look what you went through for a fucking watch. I bet you're jealous of your woman, too."

"Are you jealous of Gloria and Ted?"

"That's over," he said with certainty.

"Maybe she'll go back," I pointed out.

He thought about it, roughing the ends of his mustache. He didn't take the bait. "Maybe she will. Up to her. I don't hold any claim. But I care about what happens to her."

"I hear you."

"Good. Hear this. You cut me a break on Pike's bill. Okay, I'm cutting you one on your watch. I call us even."

"Fair enough."

"This is the end. I don't want you causing Glory trouble."

"*More* trouble, you mean. Right now, it's closing in around her."

"Any trouble. If I hear you did, I know where you live."

I turned my back and said to the garden at large, "Go pick up your dog, they'll let you whenever you want. Right now he's in a cage. They'll only board him till Tuesday."

Jimmy didn't respond. I kept going.

At his gate I stopped in the shade of the crab apple tree and lit a cigarette. The Rolex still in my sweat-slick palm, I peeked down at it, then quickly put it away in my pocket. It felt awkward there, slamming against my thigh.

I've an ironic paranoia, so I kept expecting to get mugged on the way back. Didn't happen. When I got to Tompkins Square Park I relaxed a little. I was glad to be surrounded by people again enjoying the May day.

And I had succeeded, at least in getting my watch back. Just as I'd promised.

Emerging at the other end of the park, I faced across the street to the coffeehouse where I'd begun, back at square one. I went further back, back to the photo shop on Avenue A where I'd dropped off Ted Wylie's film. My order was ready. I'd lost the receipt along with the faxes from Matt to Jimmy's sleight of hand, but my business card stapled to the envelope made claiming it a breeze.

The Vietnamese man behind the counter apologized that only seven shots developed. It was okay with me; after tax it only came to $2.87—I lucked out, I couldn't've afforded more.

I stuck the envelope—unopened—into my back pocket. I was in no rush to see the photos. Before, they were part of what I was working on; now they were only a dead guy's last snapshots. Nothing at all to do with me. I had my watch back.

I needed to get to a cash machine and replenish. There was one on Second Avenue, the corner of St. Mark's Place—what Eighth Street is in the East Village. I headed that way past a mural of tropical fish clutching steamy coffee mugs in anthropomorphized fins. Rounding the corner past a glassed-in pizza parlor, I came to a string of trendy double-duty shops. A tattoo and piercing parlor, a T-shirt and spiked leather accessories store, an astrologist/palm reader, and a skateboarders' apparel and ska music distributor. None of them were open yet. Most of their business coming from late-night adventurers.

As I stopped to light a cigarette at First Avenue, a man in a cherry-pink leisure suit and white patent leather shoes approached me carrying a Sony Walkman and headphones. His face was the brown of greasy paper bags. He looked at me through yellowy eyes and a web of red veins.

"Bum a cigarette, brother?"

"Sure."

"Hey, I'm tryina get a bottle-o-wine. Two dollars for the radio."

"Sorry, can't help you, man."

And I couldn't, not with thirteen cents in my pocket. It's liberating, though, being broke in the big city: you never feel guilty denying a handout.

Taking one of my offered cigarettes, he nodded and said, "Go easy, brother."

"You too, man."

Maybe it's why I still smoke: the connection it gives me to complete strangers, always somebody looking for a light. Our shared addiction. Our suicide pack.

I walked along St. Mark's Place, feeling good about myself and wondering how long it would last. I guess I'm always waiting for the other shoe to drop, and sometimes, if it doesn't, I give a nudge.

Toward the end of the block, I passed the Porto Rico Importing Company, the narrow shop crowded with customers, burlap sacks of roasted coffee beans, and the sound and smell of grinding. Out front on a pine bench, a young man wearing a green store apron was listening to a wizened old woman holding a blue broomhandle. Her white hair was like a fright wig and the wrinkled softness of her face reminded me of whole baked apples. The young man had short hair like a G.I. Joe and a close-cropped beard. He listened seriously to the old woman's ramblings. I wished him luck; I couldn't make any sense of her. She had a thick mysterious accent and no teeth.

Just around the corner was the entrance to the bank. Down the street hovered the neon marquee for the Orpheum Theatre, the off-Broadway home of *Stomp*.

There was no one in line at the ATMs. I stepped up to a terminal and inserted my card. My balance was $84.66, and I tottered it by four twenties, each dealt out in crisp new currency, the sequential serial numbers so fresh, the ink stood high like Braille. My transaction receipt recorded the time as 15:14.

Outside, I stood facing the intersection. Across Second Avenue was the Gem Spa newsstand: cigarettes, hundreds of magazines, and egg creams made round-the-clock. North of that, the ubiquitous Gap. On the opposite corner, Dallas BBQ, white tables and chairs set up on the busy sidewalk, diners cordoned off from the wildlife by an ineffectual plastic rope.

On my corner, a man in a knitted-stocking cap and a long flimsy beard like cotton candy had three card tables set up along the curb, selling joss sticks and row upon row of paperbacks. A. A. Fair, Margaret Millar, and Robert Bloch caught my eye, but I had a backlog of books at home to read. Maybe that's what I would do now that I'd recovered my watch, catch up on my reading.

"Every book one dollar," the ZZ Top–wannabe lazily informed me.

He didn't look like he could break a twenty, and if he could break it, then he didn't need my dollar.

I started back to my place walking up Second Avenue. In front of Veselka's Ukrainian restaurant on the southeast corner of Ninth Street another man, identically grungy, slouched behind the same sort of setup, a folding table covered with books. But as I came closer, I saw around the corner a film crew of seventeen people gathered behind halogen lamps and a 35mm movie camera slowly rolling forward along twelve feet of aluminum track. There were cables and silver suitcases, a buffet table with hot coffee and sandwiches and an ice chest underneath. Tourists and late-lunchers watched the action. Someone behind the camera yelled, "Cut."

I felt like going back to the other guy and telling him they were stealing his bit, but I was a fine one to talk, a living pastiche. I kept walking, head down, tuning out the world. I didn't notice the art-deco silver peak of the fantastic Chrysler Building far in the horizon. Ordinarily it's my favorite sight walking home.

I crossed over East Tenth Street to the Abe Lebewohl Park, named in memory of the Second Avenue Deli owner, shot and killed one morning making his deposit. Case yet to be solved. I looked up to the steeple clock but couldn't see it for the overhang of leaves. Sitting at the foot of the spiky black fence was a small lady wearing a cornflower-print kerchief round her head, her face like that of a young Gandhi. She bounced loose change in a cardboard coffee cup.

"How you doing today?" she asked me, before looking up and seeing for herself. "Oh *my*, what happened to you?"

"Accident."

"Oh, you should be lying down or something."

"Thanks," I said. I dropped her all my spare change, a dime and three pennies, guilty again with eighty dollars hot in my pocket. I hoped she wouldn't look into the cup.

Exhibiting perfect street etiquette, she didn't. (At it so long, could probably tell by the weight.) "Thank you," she said. "You have a nice day now. And take it easy."

Crossing Eleventh, I looked to my left where it'd all started the night before. Leaning against a parking meter was a young, old-faced woman, her face caked in fleshtone and sloppy red lipstick like she'd been chewing beets. She caught sight of me and immediately hustled over, jutting disjointed hipbones and swinging her arm out in front of her like a speed skater building momentum. She rasped, coming nearer, "Hey, honey, you wanna date?"

I smiled, lowered my chin, and said no, thank you, then kept walking, head down, thinking, "Not unless we can go Dutch."

I was stopped in my tracks by a pair of baggy corduroys and

two dusty, torn sneakers blocking the sidewalk, forcing me to look up along a stained Orangemen's jersey at a pimply white kid with dirt-blonde hair. No one I knew, he held out cupped hands to me, saying, "Please. Change. So's I can get some food, mister?"

A soft touch, I reached for my pocket, then remembered: only the four twenties.

"Sorry, man," I said, "don't got it."

I stepped around him and kept going.

He kept pace.

"Ohhhh, come on, man, twenty cents. I got to eat food. Only *twen-tee* cents."

"I don't have it. Sorry."

"Hey, I saw you give sumthin' to that black woman! Is it cuz I ain't *black*?"

I laughed. "Look, I really don't have it to give."

"Oh come on, twenty cents. All I wan' is twenty cents for fooooood."

I looked at him again. This time I saw it: the feverish junkie face. Unspeakably devoid of humanity, it was like making eye contact with a bacteria cell. Hungry, all right, he was hunger itself, probably Mr. Starvation when he was at home.

I said to him, "I said no."

"Oh, come onnnnnnn, you fucking yuppie."

I stopped dead and turned about and faced him. Rage vomited up from nowhere and I raised my hand. Instructively.

I said, "No!"

He walked smack-dab into me and I felt his sweatshirt's crusty letters flaking off on my hand. I shoved him back; it was about as hard to do as clearing a path through a beaded curtain *and* as futile.

The pimply kid hopped up and down, agitatedly screaming, "Don'T TouCH me, doN't ever TouCH me. AssHOle! I'll kick your FUC-kinASS you ever touch ME."

"Yeah, right."

I walked away, leaving my back exposed. Whatever was coming, I deserved it for stopping in the first place. Should've just
plowed through him.

Nothing happened though. When I got to my door and looked
back, the kid was hustling farther down the street, hitting up two
old ladies for spare change. They finally gave up some shiny quarters to make him stop following them.

The kid gazed down—intently—at the coins cradled in his
palm, as if their arrangement there foretold his immediate future.

The sight of him poured accelerant on my rage: I HATE
junkies. I hate them.

My hands shaking, I put the key in, and entered my building.
Glad to close a door behind me again, I stood in the entryway,
rattled.

On top of everything, the irony wasn't lost on me. I'd just gotten through telling Jimmy about my friend getting off heroin. But
Mark hadn't beat it alone. People had helped him. I didn't even
know how to *want* to become that kind of person, because every
time I looked inside me, I only saw: *I hate junkies.* I couldn't get
past it.

I took a deep breath and let it out again ragged.

Silly, letting it get to me. Why had it? Xenophobia? Or
recognition?

Mostly it was his face, I guess. That vacant, unanimous junkie
gaze. Nothing in the eyes but black holes, physically incapable of
giving back even a speck of light. A functional nonhuman, no
longer participant in anything, not even in the junk it fed on.

Heroin's not a shared addiction. Junkies *can't* share. Not because they don't want to, but because of the gnawing regret hours
later that they just *gave* it away. The charity of it slipping out of
their grasp remembered like acid burning off their fingerprints,
destroying identity.

I guess we most despise in others what we see in ourselves

and hate, and battle. Still, that kid had a lot to learn about sur-
viving in the city. Never ask for pity from the needy: it always
warrants contempt. Instead ask for our help. We understand
that, being wretched ourselves. And then, well, you do what
you can.

I checked my mail.

CHAPTER 11

My mail had arrived, but it contained neither of the checks. Instead, I found a flyer from Today's Man advertising 33 percent off on their entire stock of sport coats, a collection agency second warning, and a letter from my accountant explaining that "unless circumstances drastically improved" he recommended my "immediate filing of a court-supervised reorganization of debt," in short, declaring bankruptcy. My life was uniquely synchronized.

Coming into the apartment, I was shocked at first by the neatness and order, forgetting I'd cleaned, my eyes more accustomed to chaos and clutter whenever I walked in.

No messages on the machine. I went to my desk and took the Rolex out of my pocket and held it under the lamp. Stopped and scuffed, it looked like a cheap imitation of a cheap imitation, but it was my watch. Maybe that was the problem. I couldn't stand the sight of it.

I opened my junk drawer and dropped it in with the paper clips and pens and a picture of Clair I'd forgotten was there. A photo I'd taken, but I couldn't remember exactly when or where; a late summer or early fall, at least seven years ago (she had on my old blue pullover she'd later lost on the "T" in Boston). In her right hand she held a slice of pear out to me, to the camera. Her smile was sly, her cheek dimples etched deep as dueling scars. Her wide, dark eyes brimming over with soft humor and desperate love.

That was *her* problem in a nutshell. It was her fault; she loved me too completely for my own good. To completion. And I dreamt that would never change.

And got careless, daring, and I . . . looked the other way, and . . . got caught doing more than looking, playing the ever irresistible private eye, reading my own press. Now, of course, I knew better, but then I had no concept of the stakes, of what I'd casually risked, and promptly lost forever.

When she—when *it* stopped, all she'd ever loved *about* me stopped, or never was; instead just a muted reflection. She left behind her in its place nothing but the ugly empty mirror.

It was all my fault.

"It isn't *anyone's* fault, Sure," she tried explaining once more and then gave up for good. "We don't come fully equipped with a self that can handle the situations we face. We have to create ourselves as we go. Our situations create us."

I slammed the drawer shut on her sad voice in my head.

What've I created?

I went into the bathroom and splashed cold water on my face, getting Tigger's bandage over my eye sopping wet. I peeled it back and revealed an inch-long gash in my forehead surrounded by puffy yellow welts. The scab had clotted a healthy black-red. I dried my face and put on a fresh dressing, a pale-colored adhesive bandage that my hair just covered.

I tried smiling at myself in the mirror, but it took too much effort bucking gravity, so I let my lips sag back. "What's your problem? Give it a rest already."

I needed to hear someone else tell me all the sensible things I already knew, so I sat down and called Matt. This time I gave the receptionist my real name.

Matt came on immediately. "What's up?"

"I got my watch back, buddy. Do you believe it?"

"Are you shittin' me? That's great!"

"Yeah."

"Yeah?" Matt echoed. "What, I miss something? You get it back in five pieces?"

"It's all in one piece. 'Cept, well . . . while looking . . . I found some other things."

"Yeah, that'll happen. Exactly what sorta things?"

"A dead guy, boyfriend of the girl who took it."

"Ahhh-huh. And . . . ? What did the boys on the job have to say?"

I said nothing, and continued to, until nothing meant something to Matt.

"Are you shittin' me? You better have a damn good reason."

"I'm coming up with it now. It has to do with the girl."

"What, you got the hots for her? You would, her stealing your watch and all."

"She took it to pay a dog's vet bill."

"So? She's an animal-lover."

"She's supposed to have someone's missing drugs, right? But at the same time, there she is, desperate enough for money to steal my watch. They don't match up."

"Sure they do. She's a thief."

"Or being set up."

"That's her problem. And frankly, Pay, she sounds like the kind of kid who'll manage to wriggle out of it all by herself. So you stay out of it, okay?"

"Her dead friend worked for Ellis Dee Entertainment Productions."

"LSD?"

"No, Ellis like Perry Ellis, Dee like Sandra Dee."

"Okay, so?"

"Those guys last night mentioned someone named Ellis Dee. He runs raves at a nightclub called the Hellhole. Ties in nicely with missing drugs, don't you think?"

"Maybe, but I still don't see what it's got to do with you. No one's hired you. Stop poking at it. You got your watch back. These people'll get along fine without your help. Trust me! She may even be better off. Concentrate on covering your own ass."

"Thanks. I am."

"Oh, don't bullshit me, I know how you get."

"Fuck you."

"Look," he said, "if it's work you want, I'm still a man short on this wedding, but the bottom line is, this nosing-round-after-women-for-nothing shit is plain unprofessional. I think on the job now they're calling it stalking."

I opened my junk drawer, and without looking in reached for my Rolex again.

Matt was right. If I *was* just trying to keep busy, why not make a living, too? The professional thing would've been to take his wedding gig. Call back that Suffolk County attorney, take his overflowing divorce work, that's where the money was. My last year's income was composed mostly of divorce surveillance, prematrimonial background checks, testifying in palimony suits and custody cases, and locating missing fiancées and spouses. Both my life and my occupation built on a heap of lost love.

No wonder I wanted so badly to walk barefoot in murder.

I unscrewed the Rolex's stem and pulled it out three clicks—
date, day, time—freeing the minute hand. I asked Matt what time
it was.

"Three thirty-five."

"Here's the thing," I said, resetting the watch. "I know where
the girl is going to be in half an hour. I'd at least like to go check
her out."

"Hhhhh . . . Look, Pay, you don't need my okay anymore, do
whatever you want. But watch your step. I'll run this Ellis Dee
character through legal's database, get a credit profile, see what
else surfaces. Call me later, tell me you're still walking around."

"Thanks."

He hung up.

I made a fist around my watch and shook it a few times in the
air. The jeweled mechanisms creaked and swayed self-winding.
The second hand started to move again.

I slipped the watchband over my wrist and back down over the
pale tan line, less discernible after my day in the sun. I refolded
and pressed down the clasp, then shook my arm to make sure it
had caught. The weight felt awkward back on my wrist, heavy as
a manacle. Get used to it.

I checked the time. I still had about twenty minutes to get over
to Brooklyn, to the address where Gloria was scheduled to be at
four o'clock. The address? The address . . .

I didn't have the paper with the addresses—Jimmy did. My
spirit sank like something bobbled over a bridge. I felt the far-
down splash of it, a dull pang in my chest. Perfect word, *pang*. All
there is left to say.

Then, calmly, I closed my eyes and thought about it for a second, and the address came with ease: 93 Van Brunt Street. It was
all the encouragement I needed to be on my merry way. I was in a
mood to make new friends.

When I told the cabdriver to take me to Brooklyn, we were off
and surging down Second Avenue before the address was even out

of my mouth. We caught the next three traffic lights in their transition from yellow to red.

I relaxed back in the seat. Something crunched in my pocket. The photo envelope. I sat forward again and pulled it out and opened it.

Topmost in the slender packet of prints was the photo of a man's tattooed left arm. Taken too close, out of focus, the subject was fuzzy and bleached out by flash, but I could still make out the crowded lizard design that I'd seen on the dead man's body.

The second photo was of his right arm, a slightly better exposure, but still blurred.

The third was taken in a mirror, the camera's flash held up out of view, high over his head. With the camera pointed down, the angle was all wrong and it truncated him. He was shirtless, his bare skin as pearly as fishbelly. Across his bony chest was the circular tattoo of two green-and-yellow iguanas devouring each other's tail.

Ted, who was grinning at his reflection, had had a babyface. Sweet-cheeked, with an engaging, simple smile. The effect was marred only by puffy red chinks where his eyes should have been. I shuffled the print to the back.

The next two shots were taken in a darker interior, a crowded dance floor. The first was a freeze-frame of fifty half-naked people captured in mid-writhe, locked forever in the wild ecstasy of some long-forgotten beat. Some looked happy, some even rapturous. But others weren't dancing at all; they merely slouched on bent legs, holding tilted drinks and cold cigarettes—eyes shut, mouths slack, uncertain smiles disorganized.

There were recognizable types of the time and the place. Young men in waifish half-tees and Daisy Mae cutoffs, lithe nymphets in unbuttoned white button-downs and pleated Catholic school gym-skirts, stocky boys sporting ropy gold chains on muscle-bound chests, women in latex haltertops and black leather pants.

I kept staring into the photo, mesmerized as if I were trying to find Waldo.

My eyes reared up as the cab hit a pothole while charging down a Chinatown side street. When the shocks settled, my gaze steadied on the photo again and this time I saw him in the upper-left-hand corner. Not Waldo, but Stosh, the guy I'd given a milk bath.

Standing at attention, his bulk half-hidden by a girder, he was wearing a black bandanna, a black T-shirt, and black jeans. A good color on him.

I looked deep into his fat face and it became the whole photo for me, a nine-by-eleven enlargement. His lower lip was bent out. Lines raked his brow. His beady eyes focused like gamma rays aimed straight through the cattle-mass of dancing flesh. It was a look I recognized: he was a Watcher of the room, not a participant. Security. He even had a walkie-talkie antenna sticking out of his hand.

I flipped to the next photo, the same setting with some of the same people in the background, but taken from a different angle. No Stosh.

In the foreground, the photo framed three people, a man and two women. Tallest in the center was a storkish man in his early forties, wearing a cranberry satin blazer over a blue silk shirt buttoned to his Adam's apple. His shiny hair, copper-penny blonde, was cut in a Julius Caesar. No sideburns or any other facial hair except for pencil-thin eyebrows. He was looking away from the camera, gazing off in a contemplative frown, his full lips pursed.

He stood between two young women in frilly party gowns.

Or two young men dressed up as young women. Or a man *and* a woman dressed up as two women. It was hard to tell under their bouffant hairdos and excessive eyeliner.

On the right, the one who looked most like a woman—equine face and almond eyes—was a man in drag. The square shape of his hands betrayed him. Tattooed between forefinger and thumb of his left hand was a small daisy.

It was the college kid, Seth, clean-shaven and wearing a lavish platinum wig.

The other woman's features were more masculine: beetle brows, stubby nose, and a small cleft chin. She looked like a little boy who was trying on his mother's wig. It was Gloria. I'd almost missed her in the girl getup.

I flipped over to the next photo and the air in the cab seemed to envelop me.

It was a picture of Glory, alone, in Ted's place (I recognized the flower-patterned sheet draped over her thighs), and lit only by a shaft of soft early light. Sleeping on her side, one bare arm tucked under her close-cropped hair for a pillow, one freckled breast resting in soft collapse on the mattress, the other suspended, budding in a pert mound from a hairy armpit. There was no tan line below her pouty belly, just pale white skin and a tuft of mousy-brown hair in the narrow peak of thighs.

The cab stood still. I looked up quickly, afraid the driver was looking back at me, but he was busy making menacing hand gestures at a BMW's tinted passenger window.

I relaxed a bit until I saw where we were: bumper-to-bumper in front of One Police Plaza, stuck in a bottleneck for the on-ramp to the Brooklyn Bridge. Why had he come this way? Three mounted policemen in full regalia, on their way to City Hall Park, clomp-clomp-clomped by my cab window. One of their horses leaned low its huge head and peeked an onyx eye in. Sergeant Ed. I shooed him away and he whinnied back.

His helmeted rider aimed mirrored sunglasses down at me.

I held the photo closer in my lap. I don't know why. It was only suppressed evidence in an unreported homicide.

I tried to be professional, to study her features with a cold Bertillonian eye, the shape of her ears and the design of the flaming-star tattoo on her supple young nape. But her undressed flesh kept sidling into view. My eyes pored over it with an awed, childlike amazement usually reserved for fireworks displays and weeping-Madonna miracles.

I shook my head and turned quickly to the last photo.

Another one of Glo, this time awake and wearing clothes—a loose gray tank top and baggy boxers—sitting at Ted's kitchen table eating cereal and reading the side flap of a Count Chocula box. Aware of the photographer, she patently ignored his lens. As close-cropped as her black hair was, the bristles still suffered severely from bed head.

Here, more than in the other two pictures, she looked like the girl who'd stolen my watch. Self-possessed and determined. Alert and distrustful. The face of a kid, any kid, every kid.

The cab lunged forward, rocking me. City traffic flowing free again. We left behind the island and sailed out across the Brooklyn Bridge. According to the Watchtower digital clock on the opposite shore, it was two minutes of four. I was going to be late.

But I told myself, like a promise, like a halfhearted cheer, I wasn't late yet.

The cabbie took the bridge's first off-ramp through the sprawling green of Cadman Plaza, the grounds beneath its high trees rich with cool shadows like dark chocolate. We entered into the historic Brooklyn Heights neighborhood, ivy-overrun brownstones, sidewalk-umbrella restaurants, and high-priced specialty shops. A pair of identically permed women were swinging silver shopping bags. A walrus-faced man in Bermuda shorts was setting up an easel on a cobblestoned side street. A young couple were unloading a teak armoire from a hired panel truck. It was an area of the rich and retiring, the affluent and up-and-coming.

As usual, I was just passing through.

Ninety-three Van Brunt Street was in Red

Hook, farther south, a rundown industrial section by the entrance to the Brooklyn-Queens Expressway and the piers. The town-houses thinned out, giving way to matchbox-stacked apartments in white and red-brown aluminum siding, strung together by power lines from tall wooden Ts on the street, while most of New York City was connected underground.

Down the side streets, glimpses of Manhattan skyline, the World Trade Center towers, and, as we went deeper into Brook-lyn, Governors Island out in the bay.

We drove down Hicks Street until it curved by the BQE toll-booths, then turned onto Van Brunt. I had the driver take me all the way to the end, past the address. I looked over the brick build-ing as we went by. No one in its doorway or on the sidewalk out front. A five-story commercial space on the corner of Carroll. The bottom two stories vacant factory floors. The top three loft spaces with floor-to-ceiling windows facing out onto the street, the panes unusually clean in a neighborhood mostly boarded up.

The driver dropped me at the corner of Kane Street, outside an auto sales and repair garage. I lit a cigarette and walked back the two blocks. I didn't see a soul. Across the street was a wide, weedy macadam for tractor-trailers to turn around in. Farther down was Pier 11 and the corrugated steel warehouses of the Red Hook terminal. The salt-spiced air competed in gusts with ex-pressway exhaust fumes.

I looked up at 93 Van Brunt, then down at my Rolex: 4:09. I wondered if Gloria was by nature punctual or late; whether I should go up and see or wait outside and discover.

Motion in one of the fifth-floor windows caught my eye. A ceiling fan languidly turning. I was about to look away when the window was blocked by a faded-blue cloth pressed flat against the glass. It was the back of someone's shirt or dress, someone lean-ing with too much force against the high window. The gleaming surface of the long pane bowed slightly like an undulating bubble about to—

When things go wrong, the mind usually takes a second to catch up. For me, there's even déjà vu, which I read in some magazine isn't paranormal but actually the brain recovering from eye-blink amnesia.

Hearing the glass break—the crack, the unnerving rip, and the tinkling crash of shattering—it seemed to me to have all happened before, and I really should've made an effort to remember this time before the shards came raining down.

Instinct rocketed me backward, sending me in a low dive off the sidewalk and into the street. The broken glass hit pavement in a powder-splash of bright splinters.

I rolled to a stop in the road, too shocked to feel pain, but noticing something annoying in my upper arm. A long, green glass shard from a broken Heineken lying in the road. I stood up and plucked it out. Nothing spurted, a good sign it missed an artery. My cigarette was still clamped between my lips; I took short drags from it.

I looked up again. A fight was in progress. Through the jagged maw of cracked glass, I saw two men locked in each other's arms. One, blue shirt, and another man with a black T-shirt and hairy hands. I started to yell something, but couldn't think what.

Too late for words anyway.

Hairy Hands pulled at Blue Shirt, but Blue Shirt resisted, wildly pulling away, arching back, but entangled, flailing and falling over until . . .

the two men

toppled

out.

I put up my hands trying to hold them in space somehow. They plunged. Their descent a blur, a stain over my eyes, like a candid photo finish of their fall. Neither man screamed or made a single sound—no time, no breath—only a hiss before a sickening wet-kiss wallop onto pavement . . . followed by impact felt underfoot.

I heard shrieking from above. Out the broken window, a scarlet curtain flapped lazily, but I saw no one looking out.

I went to the men. One was one of those who'd beaten me the night before; I couldn't tell which one he was because he'd landed on his chin. Still, he was in better shape than the man he'd landed <u>on</u>, the man in the blue shirt.

A fair-skinned redhead, his head redder than ever with something like chunks of broken teacups mixed in with the blood and brains burst from his scalp. An eye lolled loose on his cheek like a shirt button on its last red thread.

I skirted a widening blood puddle, giving it the exact respect I would an acid spill. I even heard faint fizzing as it spread across the concrete, or my imagination.

The other wasn't dead yet. He mewled pitifully through a broken mouth, but the sound came more from his throat, a throbbing red pulpsack, like inside a squashed tomato. He was trying, trying to roll over, to get off the dead man, but half of him wouldn't respond. One leg was tucked under him at a novel angle.

I told him not to move, I'd go and get help.

Up the street by the warehouse gate was an emergency call box; I ran over to it. It looked ancient, its red paint flaking, but inside were two modern buttons labeled FIRE and POLICE. Flipping their catches, I pushed both. The more the merrier.

I saw two big men walking out the front door back at number 93. It was Stosh and the other remaining Curly. Stosh dressed in black jeans and a black Megadeth T-shirt, his friend wearing loose-fitting green sweats.

They paused at the mess on the sidewalk. Stosh shook his head and walked away. His partner, stunned, ran to catch up; anxious to get away, he got ahead, and had to wait.

I broke into a run, scanning the ground for anything I could grab as a weapon; didn't see any, but kept running. I only had to keep them busy long enough for the cops. Distant sirens were already whooping.

As I came abreast of the building, someone else ran out. A tall thin black woman with full, frizzy, wheat-blonde hair. She latched eyes on me and screamed for help.

I stopped. Stosh and the other man were turning the corner ahead. I had to—but the woman already had hands tugging my clothes and pulling me back, crying, "Help usssss."

She dragged me, tripping over my own feet, back to where the bodies lay. Stronger than she looked or merely motivated. When we got alongside, she let go and dropped to her knees in their mutual gore.

"Powers? Pow chops? Hold on, honey, hold my hand— *Powers?*"

The dead man's lips were parted, almost as if they wanted to answer but there were never the right words.

The only words I could think of wouldn't come for me either, they stuck in my throat like rolled tube socks. Finally, I said them. "He's dead." Graceful as socks, too.

She stiffened. For the first time, she seemed to notice the bulk of the man sprawled over her lover. Her long fingernails snatched down and sank deep into his beef.

She shook him as she tried to rip away flesh. His head rolled limply on his spine and he howled in agony, like a dog mangled in an automobile's wheel well.

I grabbed and tried to pull her off, but she was anchored to him. "Who is he?" I asked, letting go.

She shook her head, negating everything.

"They wanted Glo," she screamed. "They were waiting for Glo. Powers came out of the darkroom and yelled . . . Powers yelled at them to . . . he and they . . ."

She slammed her fists down on the broken man's back. I didn't stop her.

I looked around. People were gathering, the sound of screams bringing them out into the open. A couple of guys were in greasy overalls.

Down the street, a fire engine blazed, followed closely by a prowl car flashing blue strobes. Someone waved them down. The fire engine zoomed by hooting brassily, but the cruiser stopped on a dime.

Two uniforms calmly stepped out and walked over, assessing the situation. One was young and looked world-weary, the other, not much older, was just plain tired.

I looked to the bodies, then up at the high window in a pantomime more eloquent than any explanation I could have offered them. They told me to step back and I obeyed.

EMS arrived and I mingled with onlookers as more strayed over from the storage terminal to investigate. The crowd gave me good cover as a third policeman from another arriving cruiser came over and began questioning bystanders, taking names, and asking what they'd seen. I wanted to be absent for attendance.

But I had to leave casually and not right away. I lit up and smoked, and with the others gawked as the paramedics snapped on their surgical gloves and went to work.

The policemen pulled the crying woman off the man, her fingers loosely untangling from his shirt. She let them take her away, her rage dissipating into sorrow, twisting her body with crueler convulsions of grief.

The plain-tired officer said, consolingly, "Don't worry, lady. They'll help him."

She screamed and thrashed, and they had to restrain her and escort her away.

The paramedics built up a back brace around the injured man before loading him onto their gurney. He was gibbering, begging, bleeding. His life reduced to trauma, the concerns he'd sweated over the day before now blotted out by a single thought of clarity. Pain. I'd seen my fill of it—time to go. I was turning to go when . . .

Gloria, only a block away, approaching from the south, walking down the steep incline of Union Street. Twenty minutes late.

She was wearing big baggy jeans, like two different pairs sewn together, and a ribbed, spaghetti-strap T-shirt stained along her breastbone with perspiration. She had a Green Bay Packers knit cap pulled down over her ears, but I still recognized her. Maybe her walk. She lugged an olive drab duffel bag that batted against her thigh.

I flicked away my cigarette and started for her, keeping my head down.

She hadn't made the connection yet between the police cars and her destination.

Half a block away though, she stopped dead. The duffel slipped off her shoulder and plopped to the ground. She was instantly poised to run forward, but the sight of cops held her suspended by an invisible tether. She squinted, not knowing which way to go, what action she should take.

I hoped her indecision would last a moment longer, I was almost beside, her scent of patchouli spice-tickling my nose.

Gloria stepped forward. I intercepted, blocking the way with my left shoulder.

"You don't want to go over there," I said. "There's been a bad accident."

She jumped back a step, but quickly regained control. She stood her ground, and her hazel eyes stayed strictly on the activities of the police and paramedics behind me.

I told her, "Two men fell out a window."

Her neck muscles knotted. "Damn. Are they . . . are they okay?"

"One's dead. The other they're shrink-wrapping for the trauma unit. You know the people who live there?" I asked, trying to sound official—basically bored and ticked off at the same time—but it was a hard illusion to maintain standing so close to her.

In the trade, you either quickly get inoculated against failure or change your line of work. Hot leads fizzle out, slick maneuvers fall flat, and loose ends are left dangling free forever. To protect yourself, you expect only failure. It works, too, but also gets so hitting the jackpot can throw you.

I studied her grim profile. Her skin paler than I even recalled, maybe from shock. Her eyes were wide open, tense and alert, either like they were a trap or just prepared for one. Her smell of patchouli was overpowering, like she pumped it out instead of sweat.

"You live around here?" I asked her; it came out sounding glum, close enough.

"No, I'm . . . I'm on my way to the art museum."

"Oh? Funny thing, the dead guy's an artist. Powers Orloff. Ever heard of him?"

She took the sucker punch well. Her eyes darted over and jabbed mine. No recognition in them yet, but she was wise enough to know my interest wasn't routine.

Behind me, the EMS van's siren started wailing. She watched it pull away.

"You a cop?"

"Do I *look* like a cop?" I asked. Maybe I could stand to lose some weight at that.

"Then who—?"

In answer, I lifted my left arm and jiggled my wrist until the shirtsleeve dropped down, revealing the gold Rolex before her eyes.

She pieced it together by halves and zagged to her right/my left.

My nearest hand snatched her wrist on the fly, and I dug my heels in and wrenched her back to me.

"Let go!" she screamed.

"Settle down. Or we'll have company."

She bared small square teeth, but her shout was softer, like steel wool scouring porcelain. "Let go of me."

She swung back suddenly and flailed like a whip, almost breaking free. Almost.

Her leg shot up and I turned, her bony knee only hammering charley horses into my thighs. Her boot barked twice across my shin. She aimed a grubby fist at my face, thumb out to gouge. I ducked beneath it, and she grabbed a hunk of my hair and yanked.

But I didn't let go; I'd spent a long day playing tag with her, I didn't want to have to start looking again. I twisted her thin wrist, bringing her arm upright, tightening my grip to bite through some of her rage. Flexing my wrist muscles caused the Rolex clasp to pop open, the watch sliding down my arm loose as a bangle.

She tried to pry away my fingers, but finally gave up in a frustrated huff. She shook her head resignedly, ending her struggle. Her relaxing muscles loosened my hold.

She said, "I gotta go see if Valerie's okay. Please, will you, *please* let go of me?"

"If you mean the black girl, she's—"

Gloria sank to the ground using all her weight to break free.

I was ready for it and my hand fastened tighter. She hung there limp as a chimpanzee. Her dark eyes slant-drilled cold hate up at me.

"Get up, stand up," I told her, stealing a worried look back; so far we'd gone unnoticed. So far. "For *both* our sakes," I added with true feeling.

She squinted at me beneath her beetle brows. Without saying a word, she surrendered the tug-of-war. I lifted her back to her feet. My arm was getting kinda tired, and maybe even a little longer. I felt like a mother with an errant child.

I spoke sternly. "Your friend was killed by the people who are after you."

Her eyes went plastic and all her color drained away. She

went momentarily gray, like someone in a black-and-white movie, sagging in my arms. She was light enough to hold up with one hand. I wondered when she'd eaten last. She came to focusing on me.

"Let go of me," she rasped. "What the hell do you want?"

Looking directly into her eyes, I lost all my quick answers, and stared stonily.

I knew I couldn't hold on forever. I released her arm, saying, "You're it."

She pulled it to her like a bird retracting a wing. Hugging her arm to her chest, she massaged away my touch. I refolded my watchband and pressed down the clasp until it caught. I took out a cigarette and lit it, then, as afterthought, offered her one.

"I don't smoke."

"That's good," I said. "Never start."

"No shit, Sherlock. You're the dumb-ass smokin'."

I sighed gray plumes through my nose. She had the nicest way of sticking it to you. She thrilled me.

"What say we go someplace we can talk?" I said, and started past her, walking back the way she'd come.

At her duffel bag, I stopped and hefted it onto my shoulder. The light bundle was soft, with occasional hard objects floating around inside. It was army surplus circa 1970, a name stenciled in faded black between the straps: PVT. J. JOYCE, F CO. Darker pen sketches of horses and monkeys decorated it. I recognized the elongated style from the drawing pad at Jimmy's. More recent, though, were stains down one side: dry, dark-red.

She ran up, tore the duffel off my shoulder, and slung it over her own.

She asked, "What *is* it with you?"

"I'm only trying to get some answers, like who are the guys who jumped you last night and where can I find them?"

"How come?"

A laugh shot out of me.

"Let me try and explain something to you. Those three showed up here today expecting to find you. They waited. Your friend Powers protested and they backed him out a fifth-story window. He brought one of them along for the ride."

She shook her head, trying to make the pieces fit.

"Why would they kill Pow? They had no reason."

"People do a lot of things they don't mean to do, kid. I doubt either one of 'em meant to do the humpty-dumpty. What those three really wanted was you."

Her pause was as silent as a ticking clock minus the ticking. Just a sense of time being stored away in little packets, never to be reopened.

"It's your turn," I said. "What are they after?"

"They lost some drugs. They think I stole them."

"Why do they think that?"

"They're crazy, how should I know?"

"What's it got to do with Ted Wylie?"

"Teddy? Nothing. He wasn't even working that night. They fired him on Monday. I wouldn't have been there otherwise."

"Then this happened at the club where Ted worked? At the Hellhole?"

"Yeah, but he wasn't there Wednesday night. If he had been . . ."

"What?"

"I wouldn't be surprised that he did do this to me."

"Maybe he did. Maybe I should go talk to him about it."

"No! I don't want him to know anything about this, he'd use it to try and—"

"Come on, he probably—"

She shoved a quaking finger at my face. "Stay away from him."

I put up my hands and backed up in surrender. "Sure. Forget I mentioned it. Settle down. Hey, you know . . . you look hungry."

"I'm not."

"You gotta eat," I said.

Sheesh, I sounded like my mother. To counteract the effect, I quickly put on a mock tough-guy tone. (It fit me like a glove.) "Excuse me, ma'am, but when was the last time you came in contact with food?"

She didn't answer. But as we started walking again, I thought I detected the crimp of a smile.

The first place we came to was a dingy Mexican joint steamy with green-pepper juices, onion mist, and scalding jalapenos. She sat down at a Formica-topped table by the double glass doors and I went up to order. I half expected her to run for it when my back was turned, but when I looked over, she was still slouched in the same molded plastic chair. Her hat off now, she was mopping her face with it. Her spiky black hair was all slanted to one side. She looked bushed.

I carried back a lunch tray laden with bean tacos, beef tacos, a basket of cheese nachos, a side of gray-green guacamole, and two big colas. She liberally squirted all the bean tacos with hot sauce like an animal marking its territory. I like them hot, too.

We ate, me stopping after only one beef. Voracious, she kept going.

As she crunched into her third, I lit up a cigarette and asked, "You mentioned Wednesday before, said Ted wasn't working then. What happened that night at the club?"

"I don't know. I don't. All I did was wait in his office."

"Whose?"

"Ellis's. He was supposed to give me a job. I needed some money and a friend set it up, got me in to see him. But I didn't."

"Get the job?"

"No, see Ellis. I sat there staring at myself for like twenty minutes—he's got these mirrors on all the walls like a fuckin' ladies' lounge. Then the door opened up and Stosh came in. He's the one you hit with the milk last night." She grinned.

"He a bouncer at the club?" I asked.

"That's *all* he is, a goddamn doorman, but he struts around there like the Gestapo. Calls himself Head of Security. Dickhead's more like it."

"And those other two?"

"Benny and Wade. They're his staff."

"So he walks in on you and then what?"

"He freaked out, like he caught me crapping on the furniture or something. He starts screaming, 'Get out of Ellis's *private* office.' I told him I was waiting for Ellis."

She paused, took a bite, and chewed. Nice to see her enjoying the food, but . . .

"And?" I asked.

"I didn't budge." Another bite, another chew. "So he grabs me out. Only . . . I don't like being touched." It was the closest she ever came to apologizing. "When we got out in the hall, I dropped under his arms and jabbed my elbow up into his balls. Ha!" She laughed and blew tortilla crumbs onto my sleeve. "Man, he went down *boom!*"

We shared a smile.

"Then what?"

"I took off. The next day, I hear I stole something from Ellis's desk."

"Did you?"

She rolled her eyes. "Why even ask?"

"Okay. Well, what do they *say* you took?"

"Their weekend supply of Rhino. About a thousand hits."

"Rhino?"

"It's short for something, I forget what. It's a new designer drug making the rounds at the clubs."

"Never heard of it," I said. "Upper or downer?"

"Huh? Oh, a sorta speed. Ravers dance all night on one hit, have a blast. Only come nine A.M.—*yoink!*—the bottom drops out."

"Thousand hits. How much a hit?"

"Twenty."

"Twenty dollars?"

She shrugged. "It's cheaper than Ecstasy, harder, too."

"What's it look like?"

"I don't know. White powder."

"What size dose?"

"Comes in these piss-yellow micro-mini baggies, 'bout this big." She crooked her pinkie finger and showed me her bitten-down nail. I knew what she meant, I'd seen three of them imprinted with a rhino horn inside Ted Wylie's desk drawer.

"How do you take it?" I asked.

"I didn't fucking take it!"

"No, I mean, do people smoke it, snort it, shoot up, what?"

"Oh . . . They empty it on their tongues, sorta like a pixie stick, and let it dissolve."

"Have you tried it?"

"I don't do drugs."

I mulled that over and thought of something else. "What was this job your friend was going to get you with Ellis Dee?"

She slurped soda and swallowed.

"It was nothing."

"Uh-huh. Problem is your nothings turn out other people's somethings. So give."

"You're going to make a big deal of it and it's nothing. Just helping this guy. He makes the sale, takes the cash, then I go dance with the guy or girl, and pass it to 'em."

"I see, so he's off the hook and you're on it if he sells to the wrong person. Nice job, kid, ever thought of snake-handling?"

She grimaced. "Whoever's holding never has enough to get snagged for dealing."

"But you said before you didn't *do* drugs."

"I don't, but I got no problem with other people wanting to

pollute themselves, fuck up their lives. Nothing *I* dues going to stop 'em doin' that."

"Who you trying to convince?"

"Look, I needed the money, can you understand that?"

"Too well," I said. "It makes you good for lifting the stuff to begin with."

She smirked. "I don't even think it's stolen," she said. "They're all such airheads, they prob'ly missed placed it."

"How do you *misplace* that much?"

"A thousand hits would fit in your hand, man. It's small enough it mighta fallen behind Ellis's desk."

"Sure, or been knocked into the wastebasket. Or dropped into someone *else's* pocket. Either way it's gone and you're taking the blame so you can stop fantasizing this blowing over. Now, how do I get ahold of Stosh?"

"*I* don't know. He'll be at the club tonight."

"What about Mr. Dee? Will he be there, too?"

"Ellis is there every night."

"What's Stosh's last name?"

"Who knows names? Who cares?"

"I'd start if I was you. You left him in excellent position to fuck you over. He steals the stash himself and discovers it's gone after people saw *you* run off. And you aren't around to contradict. When he catches you again, he can make that permanent."

She wasn't impressed. "So what'm I suppose do about it? Cry to the cops? They'll be sympathetic."

"We could try sending the blame back where it belongs. Come with me to the club tonight and we'll straighten this thing out before it gets worse."

She laughed at me. I felt the gust of her breath in my face, tasted the hot sauce.

"No way," she said.

She was less afraid now that food was in her. What little color she had returned to her face; her boundaries were being restored. She rubbed a coarse paper napkin across her mouth, gazing through me again, the one-way glass up.

"Why don't you," she said evenly, "leave me alone? Huh? You got your stupid watch back, right? What more you want?"

I rubbed my brow, strumming the grooves in my forehead, and sighed. Suddenly I felt a lot older, like both our ages combined, about forty-nine, the year you turn fifty.

"Look, kid, I can go away, but this mess won't, not for you. It's not only about the drugs anymore. Back there your friend Valerie was shouting your name all over the place. The cops know you're involved."

"I'm not," she said, as if stating pure fact.

"Good luck selling them that with two corpses stuck to the bottom of your shoe."

"But you said the other—"

"I'm talking about Ted."

She blinked. "What about him?"

"Ted's dead," I said.

She gagged, but I wondered on what, the news he was dead or that someone else knew?

"I—I don't believe you."

"I don't believe you don't believe. Matter of fact, I wonder if you already knew. How'd that blood get on your duffel, Jimmy's duffel?"

"It's the dog's blood. Ted stabbed him when he tore through his arm. Prob'ly some Ted's blood, too, when Pike bit him. But Ted isn't dead." Steadily she shook her head no.

I shrugged, my turn to be evasive. I started bussing our table. Neither of us had touched the grayish guacamole. I carried the tray to the garbage can and slid the trash in.

Walking past her to the door, I said, "Come on."

"Where?"

"Back to Manhattan, to regroup. Think I saw a subway station a block back."

She followed me out. But only that far.

"I'm not going with you," she said, tugging her green knit hat back over her head, down over her ears.

Some people, you can't tell anything. They've got to find out everything for themselves. I got out one of my cards and a ten-dollar bill, and shoved them into her hand.

"For when you change your mind," I said. The dubiously magnanimous gesture leaving me with two twenties and some silver.

I walked away and didn't look back, I was the strong, silent type. I hoped my abrupt manner would encourage her to tag along, but when I got to the head of the stairs leading down to the F train and glanced back, she was nowhere in sight. It made me mad, I wasn't sure at whom.

Three levels below the street, a single platform divided the Manhattan- and Coney Island–bound tracks. It looked deserted. Either I'd just missed a train or it wasn't a popular station stop.

The walls were partially covered in soiled lavatory tiles, gaps between revealing brown caulking smears. Every ten feet, along either side of the concrete platform, columns of green girders, glazed by decades of overpainting, rose to the high ceiling, the underbelly of the road above. The thick air was steeped in ozone, urine-ammonia, steam, and the rot of moldy timbers.

I leaned out over the subway tracks and looked left into the dark tunnel for the headlights of an approaching train. Not sure if I was even looking in the right direction, I tried the other. At the far end of the platform, two lone figures, leaning out from the curving line of girders, were looking back at me. I went back to facing the other way, figuring they knew best.

I wished Gloria would change her mind. Any second she'd appear. Or I'd hear her voice behind me, or a tug on my sleeve, and then smell the patchouli again.

As quick footsteps closed in, I wanted so badly for them to be hers that I didn't look around right away. I didn't want to jinx it. What I get for being superstitious.

"Heeeey," a big-barrel voice rumbled behind me, "I know *you*."

The blood siphoned from my face as I whirled around way too late. He was right on top of me, his black Megadeth T-shirt converging and blotting out half my world.

I've always considered myself sort of nondescript, rather anonymous-looking, but by the clear, happy hate in his eyes, I knew Stosh had placed me instantly.

I took an involuntary step back and ate up the platform margin, my right heel discovering the edge of empty space.

Stosh advanced on me, his bald head looming like a huge misshapen toe.

I teetered, and quickly two-stepped to keep from falling over, falling in.

He spread wide his bull arms so I couldn't

duck round him. No room to maneuver, I craned to see over his shoulder for some outside assist, but the only other person in sight was his partner in the green sweats.

Following my gaze, Stosh called to him, "Benny! Go watch the stairs."

Benny didn't need to be asked even the once; he scurried away, glad to be gone.

Stosh stepped forward and nudged me, butting his chest against mine. I rocked on heels, clutching the empty air. He pressed down on me, our noses almost touching. His breath was stomach-churning, hot as it whistled down like truck exhaust.

"Did you think it was funny?" he said. "Huh, throwing that milk at me, huh? You fucked up two-hundred-dollar boots, man. I can't get the smell out of them. That funny to you?"

I didn't say—I didn't say anything—only listened for the train, wishing it would come, but not right that second. I thought I heard it, too, but it was only the cavernous echoes of traffic high overhead.

"Then this morning," Stosh said, anger mounting like a fever, "I open my wallet and everything's stuck inside like glue. All my money *and* the one photo of my dad—you fucked up the *one* photo I had of my dad, motherfucker! You think that was funny?"

"Look," I said, "you were ganged up on a—"

"I don't think it was."

He puffed out his chest and it shoved me back. I bent my knees and leaned with it, but he kept coming down. I was going over. But I could drag him down with me.

I grabbed the collar of his shirt and yanked. The cheap concert T-shirt tore apart in my hand, tattering into rag as I fell backward holding a rip of it.

The station tilted and whirled in flashes of darkness and light. I tucked into a crouch to keep from landing wide and tasting the third rail's six-hundred-volt jolt.

I splashed down on my left side. My arm flung out and my Rolex struck steel.

I'd landed in the drainage trough between the subway tracks. I scrambled to my knees. Stosh calling down, "See what happens you fuck with me?"

The drain's grate was clogged, its gritty black sludge sluicing through my fingers. When I got to my feet, I was covered in it.

I whipped round, and for three seconds knew nothing but the tunnel darkness, studying it for any sign of light. Don't panic, I told myself, nothing's coming yet.

The platform looked a lot higher from below, an imposing five-foot ditch. It was like standing in my own grave, except for the size, which was more like a mass grave just before the bodies are bulldozed in.

I had to think more positive: I was still in one piece.

A light breeze from the tunnel tousled my hair.

I stepped up onto the nearest rail, the platform came to shoulder height. I could've jumped up and hauled myself to its safety, but Stosh was policing the outer edge, hugging his arms across his torn shirt in a homeboy repose, drumming silver-ringed fingers on his bulky biceps. A happy look flowed down his face and splashed into a smile. I liked him better mad. He had me exactly where he wanted me. All that he required now was me to beg.

When I was a kid and didn't want to do as I was told, my dad used to say to me, "We can do this the easy way or we can do it the *hard* way." Usually, the ominous words alone (he had a great voice, used to work in radio) were enough to get me to back down and toe the line. Not until I grew up did it finally hit me: What *easy* way? There are no easy ways. Every way, somehow, is hard.

I slipped on a lazy voice and said, "Hope you got that outta your system, Stosh, because now, we've got business to discuss."

He didn't like me using his name. He didn't know mine.

"Who the fuck are you? And . . . what're you doing here anyway?"

"Now you're getting smart. Ask some more questions, it stimulates the brain. Ask yourself how long it's going to be before the cops nab you. They got a good description from Orloff's girlfriend."

A pinched, pained look came into his face. In his eyes, I should've been begging to be let up. Part of me wanted that, too, that exact *release* which mad terror offers in bounty. But pleading with him wouldn't get me anywhere I wanted to go.

The ground beneath my feet began to pulse dully, the sensation growing stronger or just my awareness heightening.

Stosh said, "I don't know what you're talking about."

"I saw you push those two men out the window."

"Bullshit, I didn't lay a fuckin' hand on the guy! He went nuts. Stupid asshole killed himself, and he dragged Wade out with him."

"That's better." I took two casual steps down the tracks to my left. Stosh kept just in front. The uneven ground was too mired in sludge for me to outrun him, but I might have to try it. Deep in the tunnels, some huge thing raged, gnashing steel-cylinder teeth like all-edge chewers. I laughed to cover the sound of it.

"Man, you screwed up good today, Stosh. You're down one man, the cops are creeping up your ass, and you still don't got your Rhino."

His eyes bulged. "You hump, don't fuck with me. You're in it with her!"

"See how quick your mind can work when you try? But you're still a move behind—the girl's out. I bought your shit from her this morning for five hundred bucks."

"Five hun—Holy shit, you know how much we fucking paid for that?!"

"Too bad, but it was a buyer's market, she was glad to get rid of it."

"Give it to me."

"Nhuh-uh, I don't think so. Last time a little girl took it away from you. I'll hand it to your boss at the club tonight in exchange for the five bills I paid and for five more finder's fee."

"Go fuck yourself."

"Think it over—it's a bargain. Right now you got nothing."

"I got you."

"But I don't have it on me, it's someplace safe; so make up your mind, the offer's expiring." Bad choice of words.

Stosh thought it over. That kind of time I did not have.

Sound and wind built to a commotion in the tunnel—*not* my imagination. Trash was rustling on the tracks. A potato chip bag clung to my ankle. Down in the darkness, a furtive yellow head-light ducked behind a not-too-distant bend.

"What's it going to be?" I said, unable to conceal my impatience.

His partner, Benny, came running down the stairs, jerked to a stop on the last step, took in the situation, and hung back short of the floor.

"Stosh, there's some kids coming down."

Stosh turned and looked down at me, and said, "Okay, asshole, you bring it tonight. Benny'll be working the door. Bring all of it! Don't burn me, or you'll find out why not."

A high shriek pierced the tunnel. Wheels squealed over a sharp turn in tracks.

I reached up to Stosh. "Give a hand."

"Fuck you." He said and ran for the stairs, then up them.

I took two steps and jumped for the platform. I got both elbows on it and, clinging to the ledge, strained to boost myself up. My body was sore, out of shape. My feet scrambled over the recessed wall below the platform looking for some purchase, legs only wildly pedaling.

A yellow headlight struck me in the face.

I kicked off with both legs and dragged myself up. My stomach was over. I only had to pull up my hips and swing my—

The concrete trembled as the train surged in. Too fast. Where was the driver? Why no warning horn blast or scream of emergency brakes? Thirty feet away, twenty-five. My legs still over the edge . . .

Someone gets caught this way now and then between platform and car. No impact, only implacable Train gliding by, pinching your torso snug up to the platform. Only numbness below your belt as the cars roll and roll and roll your legs over, twisting your middle up like sausage link. The durable flesh endures it until finally Train pulls out again, and you unravel, then die of sudden massive hemorrhaging.

I gave up and dropped back down to the tracks, threw my body forward and flattened out in the narrow space below the platform, embracing the slime-slick wall. I hunched my head between my shoulders, cinching my eyes shut for impact.

Train burst in, hurtling, exploding the air with one loud long thunderclap. Angry and undeniable, it vanquished the world, raining down velocity and violence, a thousand sledgehammers sledgehammering a thousand anvils a minute. A trampling tumult of twenty-eight tons skidding over ill-fitting tracks. The shock waves rode the jagged rim of my spine. Train's oppressive nearness, Train's monstrous lurching, stood all my hairs on end, the follicles stabbing like sharp metal filings.

The vacuum of air clawed my clothes. The mashing, gnarling steel wheels trying to inhale me. I huddled closer to the wall, wind whipping my hair into frenzy, strands lashing out, stinging numb my eyelids and ears.

Then . . .

Slower, slower, smoothly the wheels altered their tempo; slow, slowest, coming to a screeching jolt and hesitant . . . shuddery stop. The electric engines idle-throbbed. I opened my eyes again.

Above me, the doors slid open and light dripped through the crack between platform and car. Three young kids bounced on. Through the dense ringing in my ears, I barely made out the two-tone bell heralding the closing door. Then the crack of light disappeared and pneumatic brakes hissed canned air in my face.

The wheels turned slowly, squeaking, grinding the rails to polished silver. Train lumbered steadily, building momentum, then accelerated in a shot! and slithered down the opposing tunnel, hooting. Gone . . .

In its wake, a waxpaper burger wrapper spiraled back to earth. "D'mn!"

My voice sounded muffled, everything sounded muffled, nothing left to hear.

When I tried to get up on the platform again, my legs swung up and over with a gymnast's ease, now that the pressure was off. I rolled and rolled over until I was two feet from the edge. I lay a long time panting, my sweat-soaked shirt clinging to concrete slab like wet papier-mâché.

I stood finally and brushed myself off. Little good it did, the brackish waters had saturated my shirt and pants. I smelled strongly of the sump, but even that stink had a sweetness. I breathed it deeply. I was alive.

My heart paused on alert. Another train was coming. I heard it. Felt its heavy bass groan in the palms of my feet. Smelled the stale air it flushed out before it. My hand shot out and gripped the nearest girder, the heavily painted surface as tacky as a cold candle.

A Manhattan-bound train hurled into the station like a piston firing into its slot.

The wind hit me, passed through me, urged and shoved around me. I flinched, and my hand fastened tighter, the knuckles white mothballs.

When the train came to a complete stop and the doors slid open, I told myself to let go of the girder now. I shook sensation back into my hand, and stepped onto the subway car.

But I swore . . . after that, I'd be taking cabs for a while.

A man splattered in gutter filth is not all that uncommon a sight on the NYC subways; the other passengers hardly raised an eyebrow as I sat down, but there were several wrinkled noses. One belonged to a primly dressed, female junior-executive type reading a Tom Clancy paperback-wad. She changed her seat to the front of the moving car, upwind of me, her downcast eyes never swerving off the printed page. The time must've been after five, she was coming home from work, wearing ultra-white sneakers and carrying her shoes in a nylon-string bag.

I looked down to check the time, but the watchface was encrusted in mud. I rubbed the crystal clear. The time was five minutes to five. A lot had happened in an hour. As the train started back to Manhattan, I tried making some sense of it.

My idea that Stosh framed Gloria by stealing the drugs himself had tested poorly. His disgust at the low price I said I'd paid—five hundred dollars—was genuine; it pissed him off I'd gotten it so cheap. If he'd known my bluff, he would've laughed in my face. But he didn't, instead agreeing to pay me a thousand dollars to get it back.

So Stosh didn't set up Gloria.

But someone had. And maybe still was. It bothered me that Stosh and his crew had known where she'd be ahead of time. First, the night before waiting for her on Eleventh Street, then at Orloff's, turning up ahead of us both. Not the brightest of bulbs, they must've had some sort of directory assistance.

Out there was someone with a grudge against Gloria. Unfortunately, the only person I could think of was Ted, her ex. She'd dumped him, and had also sicced a pit bull on him that tore open his arm and ruined his tattoos. From the little I'd pieced together about Ted, he struck me as the kind of guy who'd get even. He certainly had a good clear motive for putting her on the spot. It was a shame he was dead.

But it got me thinking. What if Ted *was* responsible? He might've set the mechanism in motion and somehow got caught up in the works himself. Worth considering.

As the F train lurched over squealing wheels, pulling into the station at Broadway and Lafayette, I checked the time again. The time was again five minutes to five.

"Oh, shit."

On closer inspection, the watch's sweeping secondhand was motionless, stuck solid in the tick before three. A thin, spidery crack stretched across the crystal. Probably when I hit the tracks, maybe saved me from fracturing my wrist. I laughed out loud on the crowded car. After all I'd been through. *Guess I just can't have nice things.*

Distracted by misfortune, I almost missed my stop. I had to shove my way against the surge of people trying to get on the car, anxious to escape their jobs for the sanctuary of another weekend. No one wanted to let me off—not until they got a good whiff, and then the crowd magically parted. Not half-bad. I could almost see the allure.

I climbed up to Lafayette, and lit a cigarette. The pack was undamaged, my lucky day. Three smokes left. I pointed myself north and started walking home. According to the big clock overlooking the intersection of Astor Place, it was twenty after five.

I didn't see anybody who knew me on the way. I was glad, not up to explaining why I looked like Swamp Thing. But I did see a couple of familiar faces. One belonged to Calvin, the man who'd helped me home. He was busy outside the fence of Cooper Union's park-n-pay lot arranging the refuse from his grocery cart into an artistic display, loudly chiding his mistakes and laughing heartily at his successes. I didn't approach him, I wasn't one of his successes; probably he should've left me lying where he found me.

The other face I saw was only that, a face. Painted on the black wall of a seven-story building at Third Avenue and St. Mark's Place, the one-eyed visage of Spacely, one of the first people I met when I moved to the East Village. The huge mural portrait—the style of Matisse if he'd redrawn Van Gogh—was the remnant of a 1983 black-and-white indie called *Gringo*, a semidocumentary Spacely had lived and starred in as a junkie. (He'd never been proud of the work.) He looked like a pirate with his eye patch and earring, a long cigarette dangling from his mouth.

He was dead now, but good to know he was still keeping an eye on the place, myopically gazing west forever—or until they got around to painting over him. As I got closer, he looked down his nose in dismay at the new McDonald's they'd built below him. He'd been a strict vegetarian. Maybe Jimmy was right: "The Village ain't the Village no more."

When I got into my apartment, one message was blinking on the answering machine and a new fax from Matt sat in the receive tray, the info on Mr. Ellis Dee. I left it lying there, went to my desk, and took off my watch. I filed it away in my junk drawer with the flintless Zippos, the broken penknife, several dead batteries, and the cracked, dusty magnifying glass lying over the photo of Clair.

I lit up. I kicked off my shoes and peeled down my jeans, and left a trail of smoke, shirt, socks, and underwear into the bathroom. I started the hot water in the shower running and accompanied it on a long, welcome piss.

In the mirror, the bruises over my body were an unnatural assortment of pastels: yellow, blue, green, and purple discolorations.

The cut on my upper arm I'd got rolling in the street was small and shallow. I cleaned it thoroughly with alcohol and dabbed in stinging iodine with a Q-Tip.

The shower stall fogging nicely, I pulled back the curtain and inhaled warm, soap-scented mist. I stepped into the spray of water and let it massage me, soak me, wash away my sweat. All the strain suffered that day seemed worth it for those ten minutes.

I threw on a T-shirt and resurrected a pair of blue jeans from my laundry bag. Then sat down to read over the new fax from Matt. Pretty straightforward stuff, mostly gathered by accessing New York County public records and the Department of Motor Vehicles' network interface.

NAME: Ellis Dee. Legally changed in NY State in 1982.
BORN: Elliot Diecklicht, 09/11/53. Birthplace: Trenton, New Jersey.
ADDRESS: 101 W. 57th St. Height: 6-6. Weight: 170. Hair color: blond. Eyes: blue.

Three speeding tickets issued in Connecticut. No criminal record. No pending civil actions. Single, no children. He had a $500,000 mortgage on a home in Westport.

He was a former member of the Screen Actors Guild, 1983–85, membership lapsed. In 1986, he obtained licenses to open Vespers Restaurant at Park Avenue and East Twenty-sixth Street. The restaurant filed for bankruptcy within the year. He next surfaced in 1989 as a major investor in the dance club Utopia (in a space formerly operated as Club Abattoir). Utopia closed in 1991 after three of its bartenders were arrested on charges of cocaine distribution within the club. Dee, though never named in any indictment, left the country the same week. After a two-year stay in Europe, he returned to New York City and opened two new clubs: Mirage, in SoHo, and the Hellhole, in Chelsea.

The nightclub entrepreneur's previous year's income was reported at $380,000.

It was hard to believe he was sweating the loss of a handful of drugs; whatever it'd cost, he probably lost more each month in broken glassware. Nothing—in his tax bracket at least—to get homicidal over. I wondered how much he even knew about what was going on in his clubs.

Past six o'clock, someone hammered on my door. I peeped out and Tigger wiggled her fingers hello, her other hand balancing three coffees in paper cups. Her fingernails were painted silver today.

"I was going to leave them if you weren't here," she said. "I'm on my way to work." She was dressed in a black T-shirt and tan chinos (her garb when she worked as a sound technician, operating the board at Lincoln Center's Alice Tully Hall). Her yellow-green hair was covered by a tied red bandanna. She hadn't dyed it a new color yet, maybe she was going for the record.

I took one of the cups and sipped the coffee off the lid before peeling it back. The dark brew was liberally sweetened the way I liked it. Usually I'd smoke with coffee, but Tigger didn't smoke tobacco or appreciate its taste or smell. Finicky that way.

"Can you spare a minute?" I asked her.

"What's up?"

"I need to air out my thoughts."

"Hey, the place looks nice," she said, closing the door. "But, uh . . . what's that *smell*?"

She was standing beside the pair of jeans that got soaked in the drainage trough. I kicked them across the floor to the bathroom.

"I went spelunking this afternoon," I said. "Long story."

She sat down to listen to it, first sitting on one leg, then crouched on both ankles, then with her feet flat on the floor. I gave her the *Reader's Digest* version, surprised how little there was to tell. Then again I had to leave out the part about finding Ted's body. Officially, I hadn't.

She knew some of the people mentioned. It didn't surprise me Jimmy was one of them; she'd actually helped clear out his garden and till the soil.

"He's got a beautiful place there," I said. "How is he able to keep it?"

"It's on city-owned property, and right now they aren't doing anything with it. He's okay until investment potentials move farther east. *Then* they'll go after his place, like all the other homeless settlements in the city."

"What kinda guy is he?"

She looked at me. Caramel eyes hardening into cold chunks. "He's a friend of mine, Payton."

"I know, that's why I'm—"

"I'm not going to tell you anything. He's someone I care about. He's had trouble in his life, but now he's got his shit together. Don't do anything to hurt him."

"What could hurt him? No, really, what? I'm just trying to get answers."

"I don't know, I'm not comfortable talking to you about him. Please stop."

"He told me he's checking into a drug treatment program on Monday."

"Good."

"How bad is he?"

She stared me down, her lips stiff white chalk.

"Okay," I said. "But one question, would you say he's a violent guy?"

"Anyone can be violent. When provoked." She made it sound like an intimate threat. "But if I were you, I'd watch my step with him. He's a serious man."

"Fair enough." I moved on.

She knew Ellis Dee, but not personally.

"Met him once, few years back, did sound for a concert he produced at the Palladium. I liked him. Stayed out of everybody's way, let us do our job. You'd be surprised how rare that is."

"No I wouldn't. Ever been to his club, the Hellhole?"

"Yeah, a few, Ez mixed the house there a couple times."

"What's it like?"

"Big. Built into an old Methodist church on West Twenty-first."

"A church?"

"Only the building of one now. But since it used to be a church, it already had all the public-assembly permits you need to open a club. Not that unusual really. I wired a church in Philly, club called Revival, in Old City, same deal. The Hole's popular right now as a multilevel meat market. Ez can't stand it. He prefers venues where he has a closer relationship with the crowd. The Hole's too schizophrenic for him."

She didn't know anyone who worked there.

I described the two clubkids, and she knew Droopy. It seemed he had a slight fame in the clubs, everywhere you went everyone seemed to know him. She'd even partied with him a few times.

"But there's not much there to get to know, if you know what I mean." She tapped her forehead. "A huffer."

"A what-er?"

"Huffer, like 'huff and puff and blow your house down.' He's hooked on inhalants. Don't ask me why, kills the brain cells."

I recalled the chemical smell I'd gotten off his breath at the sushi bar.

"What kind of inhalants?"

"High-end, you've got ether, amyl nitrite—the stuff they use for heart attack victims—and nitrous oxide, laughing gas. Also used in whipped cream canisters."

"Whippets I've heard. And those popper vials," I said.

"Yeah, right. Low-end is pretty pathetic. Some start out sucking gasoline fumes or spray paint, bottles of cleanser and paint thinners, anything to vaporize the brain. Highly unglamorous addiction."

"What about this Rhino stuff, more attractive?"

"Infinitely."

"So you've tried it?" Wasn't really surprised.

"Couple times, relatively new, a specialty drug," Tigger said with an air of authority. "It was originally developed by this pharmaceutical outfit, Fer-Nel Labs, as a motion sickness relief. Instead their chemist stumbled on a new hallucinogen. Its chemical name is Ryno-thylene-dioxy-amphetamine."

"Vega-meata-vita-mina-what?"

She smiled thinly, then repeated.

"Rhino for short. One hit gives you this aphrodisiac high that lasts for hours. On top of that, you can spin around in circles without ever getting dizzy. Great for raves. Coming down is a little rough though. The slogan-buzz is, 'It keeps you charging all night, then turns around and gores you.' "

It rang a bell. I'd overheard Seth say something similar on his digital phone. I described the NYU student to her, but she couldn't place him at first. I got out the packet of photos and showed her the one of him in drag. Isolating his face with her thumbs, she slowly recognized him.

"Oh, yeah, right. Droopy's shadow. Recently acquired. That must've been at some Wigstock after-party, I don't think he's a queen. I got the impression he was some slumming rich kid. Always buying rounds. Tries too hard to act the host and gets on people's nerves. Usually ends up sitting alone while Droopy's off doing business."

"Business?"

"He deals a little."

"Droopy's a drug dealer?"

"Nah. Well, you know. When you do drugs, you become a sorta conduit for all kinds. But he probably uses more than he'll ever sell."

While I had them out, I showed her the rest of the photos: Ted Wylie and his tattooed arms (didn't know him); the crowd shot with Stosh in the background (didn't want to know him). I held back the one of Gloria half-naked in bed.

Naturally, Tigger picked right up on it. "What's that?"

I gave it to her to see.

"Dirty old man," she scolded.

"Since age eight and a half."

"Is this her? Gloria? The one who stole your watch? She's cute."

I didn't know what to say. I asked, "What should I do about her?"

"Sounds like you've done enough. Too much. You offered to help her and she told you no, right? Well, you can't beat a dead horse."

"Sure you can, you can beat it into the dust."

She frowned. "But it doesn't do any good."

"Sometimes it makes you feel better."

"And drains all of your energy."

"I don't have much choice now anyway. I've got to follow through on this meeting tonight."

She stared me straight in the eye.

"Why?"

"Because if I don't they'll go after the girl again, only this time to get to me."

"Bullshit, you don't believe that. Wait a minute—did you just say 'the girl'? Man, you're really eating this up, aren't you?"

I wanted to protest, but the breath to make the words vocal stuck in my chest. Maybe she was right. What if I didn't show at the club, what could Stosh do? He didn't know my name or where to find me. His chasing after Gloria had proven expensive, at least in human life. And now that the police were involved, it was wiser for him and everyone to keep a low profile. Time to cut losses all around. But I wasn't ready yet.

"You know," Tigger said, "I think you may be like those sea creatures that can only live in turbulent, sulfurous waters—you need frenzy to survive. My older brother's like that, a racecar driver down Daytona. A real adrenaline-seeker, only feels alive when disaster's coming at him round the next bend. But adrenaline's got a reason, Payton. Don't go seeking it out like a junkie. It makes you reckless."

"Point taken," I said. "Thanks."

"Do you hear that?"

A low buzz was coming from the desk in front of her. I pushed aside some papers to reveal Gloria's small black beeper. Forgot I still had it. I checked the incoming call. It was the number to the digital phone, either Seth or Droopy calling. I wondered which and why.

I asked Tigger if she'd answer the page for me, explaining, "It's got to be a *woman*'s voice."

She took the beeper from my hand and read the number. "What should I say?"

"As little as possible. They'll be expecting Gloria, so only say hello."

She started dialing then stopped.

"What if—"

"Don't worry," I said. "You can't be any worse than my mom."

"Huh?"

I pointed to the phone. She started dialing again. When she

nodded, I picked up the receiver on my fax machine and listened in. The number was ringing.

A crackle of wind answered, followed by a clipped hello.

Tigger said hello back.

"Glo?"

"Uh-huh."

"Who the hell you giving this number to?" Seth's voice, screechy and rattled. Sounds of traffic in the background—he was mobile, outdoors somewhere.

Tigger improvised a "Huh?"

"Some dickhead called this morning, said he had a bag of your stuff. It turned out to be nothing but junk. He asked us a lot of questions about you and Ted. And now your friend Jimmy just called, all fucked up, babbling all this whacked-out bullshit. Look, I don't know what's going on, but keep *me* the fuck out of it. Tell your junkie friends to stop calling me!" He broke the connection.

I listened to Tigger's breathing mingled with dial tone. Echoes sinking in. She put down the receiver.

"Tig, I—"

She pushed past me. "I'm late for work."

"Tig, wait . . ."

She paused at the door. I could see the remark about Jimmy had upset her: her eyes boiled with mute accusation. "What?"

"I'm sorry."

"What for? People make their own decisions. You be careful making yours."

The apartment's reinforced-steel door clanged shut behind her.

CHAPTER 16

I lit up and smoked. One cigarette left.

I called Matt to let him know I was okay, even though at the moment it was a toss-up. I'd been exhibiting a level of professionalism you could stub a toe on. The receptionist asked me to hold, Matt was on another line. Friday evening, almost seven P.M., but background noises of office life at Metro Security were hectic. Most of their real work started after dark. They never slept.

Me, I needed a nap, feeling drowsy coming down off the adrenaline rush of near-death. Waiting on hold, I felt my eyelids droop, my head bobbing like a seed-heavy sunflower. I shook it off, finished my cigarette, then slurped the cold dregs of my last coffee.

Matt's voice intruded on my limbo.

"Hey, how'd it go? Did you see her?"

"Who?" I thought he meant Tigger for a second. "Oh, yeah. Yeah."

"You okay, buddy?"

"No, I'm fine."

"Did you get my fax?"

"Yeah, thanks. But sorry I put you to the trouble, I've decided to let it alone."

"Are you shittin' me?"

"Yeah, I'm out."

Matt waited for the rest. I would've obliged, but my thoughts were as blank as bedsheets drying on a clothesline, evaporating watermarks and changing shadows.

Matt said, "Good for you! Finally some sign of maturity. Glad to hear it."

His sarcasm was unexpected. What ax was he grinding?

"Look, she doesn't want my help," I said. "And like you said, she might be better off. There's been another death."

"What?! Who?"

"The guy in Brooklyn, Orloff, had an accident out his fifth-floor window."

"You didn't push him, did you?"

"No, they started without me. But thanks for asking."

"Who did it?"

I told him what happened. And as I did, I couldn't escape the feeling that my hand had somehow pushed him, that if I'd stayed in bed that morning, he might still be alive. I explored that feeling. I knew of at least one person who'd known about Gloria's four o'clock appointment in Brooklyn. The time had been written under the address on the faxsheet Jimmy took away from me. But that only confused me more; I believed he'd rather die than do anything to harm Glory.

"So," Matt said, "I throw out the rest of this stuff I got on Dee?"

"What's that?"

"Well, thought what I faxed before stunk of antiseptic, so I called some friends on the job. You remember Dove Wright, used to work out of Manhattan South, retired last year? Well, Dove knew all about him. Even got a little antsy me asking."

"What'd he say?"

"Both of Dee's clubs were raided twice in the past year for narcotics distribution, but the raids turned up nothing 'cept the stuff lining a few customers' pockets. Planned raids, built on solid inside information, but when the cops arrived, the targeted dealers were home watching TV. As if somebody got the heads-up."

"Dove told you that?"

"Are you shittin' me?! No way. But he did his best not to."

"Takes a lot of juice for that kind of public assistance."

"You're telling me. But this Dee guy's tied into a lot of money-making ventures. He's got plenty to throw. You might've finally hit some pay dirt, kid."

"What do you mean?"

"What do you think I mean? He operates two nightclubs, owns a house in Westport, he's a big event-organizer. He obviously needs the services of a good—"

"You're eyeing him as a client?"

"What else? But not for me, you bastard, for you. I got too much work as it is."

"He's a crook."

"Don't discriminate. Crooks need security, too, *more* so. Anyhow, most of his business looks legitimate. And he pays his bills. Can you say that?"

"What about his drug ring, doesn't that bother you?"

"You aren't sure yourself how much he knows about what's going on in his clubs. And after your description of Stosh and the others working for him, I figure he could use someone to go in and clean house. Monitor his employees, find out who's milking the till—and maybe who's operating a separate business out of his club."

"I see what you mean," I said. "But . . ."

"But what? Your *scruples*?" Like it was a foreign word used only by foreigners and phonies. "You can't afford 'em."

"They're all I can afford—I own them outright."

"Pose later, Pay. I'm just trying to turn your little sleuthing spree into some green. These are the ground balls you gotta snag standing in the outfield."

"I know . . . I appreciate you pointing out the play, really. Guess I'm just tired."

"So sleep on it. Who's rushing you? But keep me posted."

"Okay. Thanks, thanks again. Give my best to Jeanne."

"You haven't got it to give, bud."

I hung up the phone.

The light was still blinking on my answering machine. One message.

I wondered who, ticking off possibilities, long shots and favorites: Gloria, a bill collector, my mom, Tigger or Matt (and neither mentioned it), my dentist reminding me of my six-month cleaning, the Chungs telling where they'd gone, and, astronomically remote, Clair calling me to say, "Hey, how are you? I had this feeling you were having a bad day." When I would have settled for merely hearing her husky breath on my line again.

If I wanted to hear her that badly, *I* could have called, I knew her new number. Not that she ever gave it, but it's what I do. She'd take my call, hear me out, reasonably listen to all my reasons. But that was worse than a hang up, like it was all my hang-up.

I would never call her. She would never call me.

I pounded the PLAY button as if it were labeled SELF-DESTRUCT.

"Hi, this is Roxanne from the animal hospital. You asked me to call if Gloria came by for Pike. She did. She was surprised you paid so much of her bill. . . . It's five-thirty now, Friday. We close

at eight, if you need to speak to me or, *well,* if you feel like going
out for a drink later . . . ? You have my number. Bye."

Hadn't seen that one coming. It seemed to offer more proof of
how off my game I was. I needed to restore energy. I ordered myself, "Drop and give me twenty winks."

I went and lay down on the couch, just to rest my eyes for a
few. I listened to the muffled rhythms of the city going on around
me and drifted off, then back again.

I dreamt I was a clam, embedded in sand thousands of fathoms
below the sea, who suddenly felt the weight of the entire ocean
pressing down on him, forgetting it was just his world all around.

I startled awake, eyes opening to a photo-negative of the room
I'd fallen asleep in. It felt like only seconds had passed. Where before had been light around me, it was inky black, and where faint
shadows stood in corners, orange streetlight now blazed as bright
as an electric-heater element. I'd overslept by five or six hours,
deep into night. My telephone was ringing.

I answered it before the machine did, my ear meeting waves of
confusion. Fire engine horns honking like angry dragons that
then dopplered going by. A dog barking savagely, and a small,
thin voice commanding it, "Settle down, settle down, Pike."

"Hello? Hello," I said.

"Mr. Sherwood?" Her mouth was pressed too close to the receiver, her breath zuzzing. "This is Gloria. You know—"

"Yes. Where are you?"

She didn't answer. In the background, Pike whimpered a
stream of howls. Something was wrong. I slapped my face until
the sting brought my eyelids full up.

"Gloria, are you okay?"

"They killed Jimmy. They killed him. Fucking killed Jimmy."

"Gloria, where are you?"

"They—we were only gone an hour. I took Pike for a walk and when we came back the shack . . . on fire. They set him on—"

Horns blasted by, gobbling and garbling her words.

"—but I couldn't get to him. Pike went in, I had to drag him away. They killed—"

"Who?"

The berserk baying of sirens whooped and cackled, deadening her response.

I shouted quickly, "Gloria, where are you?"

"Down from Jimmy's."

"I'm coming there, stay nearby. Don't wander. I'll be there in five."

"I didn't think they'd—I didn't know. I didn't know."

"Stay put," I said, and waited for an answer, but the connection broke.

The first cab I flagged wouldn't take me over there. I lied to the second cabbie about how far east we were going, saying only Avenue B and Tenth.

Nightlife in the East Village on Friday was as flashy and frantic as the last days of Pompeii. Roaming herds of people released from late movies crossed paths with revelers only just breaking the seals on their night. Up and down the avenue, the volcanic glow of streetlights bathed the sparkling asphalt in a vibrant orange wash. The white headlights of traffic were like a lava flow gaining on us. Abruptly, the cabbie changed lanes to the far left, and we shot down Tenth. The side street was a cooler dark, with low, leafy trees blocking the artificial light all the way to Avenue B.

As I urged the driver farther east, I could smell the acrid air. Dense wood smoke, growing thicker as we turned south onto Loisaida. Ahead of us, the ricochet of blue-strobes and revolving-red lights. Ninth Street was closed off, congested by fire trucks and cruisers. A stream of black water gushed along the curb and into the sewer.

Activity was centered halfway up the block outside Jimmy's garden, lit up by lightning-intense klieg lamps mounted on a fire truck. I paid the cabbie, got out, and walked over. A crowd was penned back by yellow caution ribbon. A mass of dense brown-gray smoke hung low and menacing overhead like the Hindenburg about to crash. My eyes stung, smarting from the sharp air. Far-flung ashfluff falling back glanced off my cheek.

I worked my way through, looking for Gloria, scanning the faces transfixed and transfigured by the spectacle, some fused in horror or grief, others bored, detached, like eyes waiting for an elevator. I caught bits of conversation, people speaking in humble mumbles as befitted the dead, some voices in Spanish: *"hombre . . . incendio . . . muerto."*

A few firemen stood in the street smoking cigarettes and gabbing. The fire had been extinguished. One hose crew still operating from the parking lot next door shot water through the chain-link fence onto the pile of charred wood at the back of the lot, where Jimmy's shack had been. Men in big rubber boots and black-and-yellow turnout gear raked the smoldering rubble with pry bars. Two of them lifted a collapsed section of wall and a small fire erupted, quickly squelched by the hose crew.

One man holding up the wall hollered out, "We got one here!"

A young police officer and two fire marshals went to investigate, ignoring the garden path and walking across some tulips. They were already mashed anyway.

The firemen cleared away the wall, then crowded their discovery, heads bowed low like penitents, or drunks pissing in the snow. After a while, the fire marshals squatted down and poked the steamy ashes, jotting down notes in palm-held pads. They stood and brushed off their pants. One of them came back, talking with the uniformed officer.

I moved to where I could eavesdrop as the fire marshal asked the policeman if he knew who had called in the 1041, the code for a suspicious fire.

"Sheriff's unit spotted the smoke, called us and FD," the officer said. "I notified you guys because the crowd was making noises about it maybe not being an accident."

"Any of them see anything?"

"No. Most came after the trucks."

"Anyone live around here who might have seen what happened?"

"Maybe squatters farther down, but the block's vacant. My partner's asking around."

"Uh-huh. Anybody know this guy?"

"Yeah, name's Jim. Been living here since before I been working here, three years. Planted this garden, built the shack. He was a junkie. Never trouble though. Stepped in, couple times I know of, smoothed out a situation. Okay guy. Too bad."

"He live in there alone?"

"Far's I know. Think he had a dog."

"Well, one of 'em must've knocked that heater over. Cool enough night for it. There's wax, too, so Jimbo had a candle going, maybe cooking up a spoon and got careless. Out of it, that's for sure. No scorching underneath him. The place went up like a book of matches. All that scrapwood covered in paints and varnishes, it all fed the flashover. Roasted him blacker than—"

"Hey!" I shouted—heard myself shout—"You don't think this was an *accident*?"

The men looked without turning their heads. The fire marshal was tall and wide. Bushy brown hair and a bushy brown mustache. He had hockey goalie eyes that made me feel like a puck.

The cop had a more relaxed expression; he was used to the open forum of the East Village.

They spoke again, dropping their voices. The fire marshal left and rejoined his partner, kicking through ashes. The police officer came over to me, his hand resting on the butt of his firearm. He had a square upper torso and long legs. He looked about five years younger than me and twenty pounds stockier. His name tag said GORRINO.

He requested I step back from the line, then asked me if I'd seen what happened.

"No, but I knew the guy. He wasn't stupid. And he was off the junk. He wouldn't have been careless with the heater."

"What's your name?"

"Gus," I said.

"You saying he got torched, Gus? Do you know somebody'd who want to?"

I thought the length of a pause, then shook my head no. I'd tied my own hands not reporting Ted's death. What else did I have to go on except Gloria's frantic phone call? And she was nowhere in sight.

Officer Gorrino said, "Look, those guys know their job. If there's anything to find, they'll find it. Don't make trouble. Why don't you move along? Go home."

Two men from the coroner's office approached carrying an aluminum-and-nylon stretcher. The first man ducked underneath the yellow police ribbon, then on the other side held it up high for his partner to duck under.

Ashes, ashes, I thought, *we all fall down.*

They carried the stretcher to the back, and returned shortly. What they carried back, wrapped loosely in four-ply plastic, was only a charred effigy of a man, shriveled into a fetal position, his muscles contracted and his skin blackened.

I had to find Gloria. Fast.

I crossed to the other side of the street and circled round the back of a fire engine where people watched at a more discreet distance. This group was made up mostly of street people dressed in browns and soiled-greens. No Gloria.

I saw a short, stocky woman in black with a Minolta slung around her neck and a camcorder in her hand, videotaping two men. One of the men was a rangy kid with grimy dreadlocks, splotchy skin, and ring-pierced eyebrows, nose, and lips. The other was much older and more remarkable-looking. Six feet tall, barrel-chested, dressed in a sharkskin suit tight in the shoulders and crotch. A natural redhead going to timely gray. His large, lumpy face had red-and-gray eyebrows, like raw cotton dipped in paprika, and a shiv-stiff, waxed red Vandyke.

Closer, I heard him questioning the younger man.

"When did you see Jimmy last?"

The kid said, "I walked by round nine tonight and he was outside playing with his dog. He had a big plastic cone round his neck—the dog, I mean. Guess he got hurt. This black-haired chick was with him. We waved. That was like nine . . . or maybe ten. Dark already, I know that."

The big man's manner was as refined as a five-star maître d's. He asked, "And at what time did you first see the flames?"

"Like a half hour ago, we were hanging in the park when the cherry-poppers go by. So we checked it out. Man, the place was cookin'. The air like all wobbly from the heat. All these orange snake tongues shooting out of the cracks, and then like— *whoosh*—one of the walls cracked open, man, and fire, man, was everywhere. A wicked cool flameball erupted right on top. Awesome. Scared d'shit out of me."

I got too close to them and when I looked up, the short woman was no longer recording the men, but aiming her camcorder at me. She was Asian, in her late twenties/early sixties, with a chubby, pleasant face that keenly reminded me of Mrs. Chung's. I wondered, was she Korean?

As I leaned to get out of the shot, she lowered the camcorder and smiled apologetically.

"Hell, I'm sorry, I forget sometimes I'm even holding the damn thing. Usually, I think to ask first, sorry."

Her fluent American surprised me. "No problem," I said, turning to walk away.

"Hey, did you know Jimmy?"

I was about to tell her no, when the big man in the sharkskin suit came over, a broad toothy grin on his face.

He asked the woman, "Who have we here, Hi-K? Another friend of Jim's?"

I started to deny it, but he wouldn't let me.

"Terrible thing, sad. My name's Declan Poole, by the by."

He held out a big pink bearpaw and wrapped it around my hand.

"My name's Payton," I said, "but I'm not a friend. I was only passing by."

I looked to Hi-K for confirmation, but she had her camcorder up again, videotaping me. I raised an eyebrow.

"Oops," she said. "Sorry, force of habit." But didn't stop recording.

Declan drew back my attention. "I edit *The Weekly Cause*. It's a neighborhood paper. Do you live in the neighborhood, Payton?"

"Yeah."

"Then you must've seen a copy. Hi-K's my photographer. *And* bodyguard," he added, smiling slyly.

She lowered the lens to return his smile, and I was struck again by her resemblance to Mrs. Chung. It gave me an idea, the first of few.

I got out my wallet and the copy of the note I'd found at the deli.

She zoomed in on it.

"Could you read this for me?" I asked. "Um, translate it, I mean."

Her mouth frowned, disdainful. "That's Korean," she said. "I'm Chinese. You think we all the same, Joe?"

I pulled back, apologizing, but she stopped me.

"Hold on—I didn't say I *couldn't* read it. Just making the point."

Declan explained, "Hi-K's actually Dutch, born and raised in Holland, but she speaks and writes nine languages fluently."

Hi-K looked at the four columns of script, then pronounced, "A woman's writing. Let's see." She mumbled a few words in Korean, then, disappointedly: "Oh, it's only a note to a beer distributor, telling him they've gone out of business and moved away."

"Moved? Moved where? Does it say?"

"I think . . . says Vancouver."

Then it hit me. Mrs. Chung had mentioned once she had a sister in Canada who ran a chain of photocopy stores. "One day we go," I remembered her saying, in English more precise than I ever gave her credit for. One day had come and they'd gone.

I thanked Hi-K and took back Mrs. Chung's note, refolding it and putting it in my wallet where pictures of the wife and kids would normally go. Knowing the answer didn't make me feel any better—a lesson I never fully learned.

Losing interest in me, Declan Poole wished me good evening, and moved off to find more talkative fare, Hi-K's steady camera-eye panning in pursuit. I still had to find Gloria.

At the corner of Avenue D was a lighted pay phone. I headed for it, walking under the scaffolding of the corner building under construction. From the gloom of its dusty entrance, a voice barely risked being heard.

"Mr. Sherwood?"

I turned to look, the darkness was impenetrable. The abandoned building's hall exuded a wet-clay dank. I took a step into it, whispering her name, "Gloria?"

A ravenous growl at ankle height responded, hot breath seeping through my pant leg and sending the hairs up on end.

"Gloria?"

She stepped out, her face catching streetlight, gleaming eyes puffy and cheeks smutted. A tear rolled down her face, diminishing and disappearing over the dark line of her jaw like a shooting star. Her lips were azure—not blue lipstick.

She was holding Pike by a dirty nylon leash wrapped twice around her hand. The dog looked like a broken toy, soot-faced, his lampshade collar melted down to a broken hoop around his neck. His whiskers were singed, shriveled to black nailheads.

I reached out for him to sniff my hand, but his wet snarl stopped me. I drew back.

Gloria warned, "He's protective of me."

"I see that. Are you okay? What are you doing over here?"

"People were asking—they saw Pike and they wanted to know what happened to Jimmy. Someone had a camera. And then the police came and started asking, too, so I hid here."

I wanted to ask, too, but that cold dark entryway wasn't the place. She looked shaky on her feet, so I backed down.

"Please come with me," I said.

She flung up her head and edged back into a shadow. "Where?"

"Away. Come on. Does it matter?" I waved my hand toward me in a circular motion, as if I could draw her out as easily as a fragrance.

From the gloom she asked, "Why did you come?"

"*You* called *me*. Remember?"

"And what do you want for it?"

I sighed. "Do you really think you're the first person to ever have the world fall on 'em? You're not alone. I've been there plenty myself, and I never got out from under it *alone*. Somebody always stepped in and helped—don't ask why, I don't even know. Sometimes people I knew, but lots of complete strangers, too. You've got to give that back in kind, the only way you can. That's all."

Nothing else was said, but slowly Gloria emerged into streetlight again. We started walking toward Avenue D together, Pike stopping and sniffing every few feet at a street sign or lamppost.

It wasn't a place to catch a cab ever. We walked up a block, then over two, heading west along barren streets glowing like molten copper. The ghosts of sirens—monosyllable screams like communicating cats—floated high in the night air, answered back by uptown and down, westside and Brooklyn.

I noticed Gloria's right sleeve was burnt to melted fragments, the hair on her arm singed. A bubbly patch of blister forming on her right hand. She smelled strongly of wood smoke. It erased completely the patchouli.

I asked where her duffel was. She didn't say anything. I reached for my cigarettes, but only one left so I saved it. After half a block, she finally answered dazedly. "Left it at Jimmy's."

"What happened there tonight?"

"I told you before, I don't *know*. I don't—"

"Look, I know you've gotten a raw deal, but the only way to stab back is not to take it lying down. Don't flinch when you're slapped and don't duck under the blows. Now, on the phone you said you took Pike for a walk; what time was that?"

"I don't . . . Ten maybe."

"How long were you gone?"

"An hour, two. When I got back, I saw all this light coming from the garden. I . . . I thought first he was burning trash, but it was so bright."

"Was anyone around?"

"No, I didn't see. I got closer, and this black smoke was—I ran, the flames were shooting out of Jimmy's shack. All fire! Like a wall of fire. Pike got away from me and ran right at it. I had to drag him out. Crazy, he almost bit me. They *killed* Jimmy."

"Who, Gloria?"

"You know."

"Stosh? For Ellis Dee? I doubt it. They've got enough troubles right now."

"It had to be."

"I don't think so. If this has anything to do with anything, Gloria, it's Ted's murder. Do you know who killed Ted?"

"No."

"Did Jimmy? Is that what happened? They had a fight over what Ted did to his dog and Jimmy killed him?"

"No."

"Why was he so nervous today? Was he using again?"

"Jimmy wasn't using."

"That's not what your friend Seth said."

"That prick? He's no friend. Just some college kid Droopy's been leeching off of, squatting at his dorm. Nothing but a parasite."

It sounded more symbiotic to me, but I let it pass. School was definitely out.

I said, "Seth got a call from Jimmy this afternoon, said he sounded out of his head. What happened to upset him?"

"I don't know."

"Glory"—I deliberately used Jimmy's name for her—"let's talk straight. That must've been about the time you brought Pike home. What happened?"

"Nothing. I just told him about Powers. And about *you*, and what you told me about Stosh killing Powers, and about . . . Ted being dead."

"Was that news to him?"

She didn't answer.

"Hey, you didn't hear the fire marshal back there. He's writing your friend's death off as an accident. Just another junkie who flew too close to the flame."

"Jimmy wasn't—"

"Doesn't matter. What difference you think it makes to them? This way it's neat and tidy. A lot less forms to fill out than a homicide. Everyone's happy, except for maybe people like you, a segment who haven't the pull in this city to use a public toilet."

"They murdered Jimmy."

"But to get the cops to see it that way, we've got to bring them something more."

She walked four stiff strides.

She said, "Jimmy got in this real weird mood, real quiet. He picked up the hoe and started swinging it, cutting down plants. I asked what was wrong, it was like he didn't hear me. Then . . . he told me . . . he said he'd make them *stop*, that if they didn't leave me alone, he'd go to the cops about—"

"About what?"

"He said he saw who killed Ted, he was there the morning it happened."

"At Ted's apartment? When was that?"

"Dawn on Thursday, he was looking for me and Pike. I hadn't seen him yet or told him what happened. Not until that afternoon. I . . . I waited too long. He was out of his head. He went over there thinking Ted killed us or some . . . When he got there, Teddy had company, so he waited in the hall. After they left, Jimmy went in and found him, then got the hell outta there."

"Was he sure Ted was dead?"

"He didn't care. Jimmy hated him for hitting me. He said he got what he deserved, that it didn't matter who killed him."

"Not until tonight," I said.

"That's because of *you*, you came looking for me, asking questions about Ted."

"Would you rather I ignore it? You lived with him. Did Ted deserve getting his head bashed in, suffocated by a plastic bag?"

"Is that how he—"

"Answer me, did he deserve to be executed?"

She shrugged. "Maybe. I don't know."

"You lived with him, you must've loved him once."

"What are you talking about, man? It was *winter*, and he had a *bed*. We weren't Romeo and Juliet!" Her anger made Pike prick up his ears and growl at me. "I'd meet him outside the club after closing, go back to his place, fuck if he still could, then sleep till he kicked me out in the morning. Sometimes he snuck out a side entrance and left me in the fucking cold all night! What the fuck do you think it was? Love?"

"Quit it," I said.

"Why don't you grow up?!"

Her voice sounded older and harsher now; I wondered whose it was. Maybe it'd been a favorite rant of her mom's. Or maybe one of Ted's. But where had they gotten it?

We were coming to the corner of Avenue B and Tenth, not a place for a scene on a Friday night, too many people out and about even at that late hour. On the opposite corner was a popular sidewalk bar and café. A couple of cabs waited outside it. I flagged one over, and it made a broad, illegal U-turn and stopped at the curb.

Gloria asked, "Where are we going?"

I was thinking emergency room, but I said, "My office. We need to put cool water on your hand. How's it feel?"

Blisters had formed like a wax glove over her fingers; the burn looked like it could be second degree, but I was afraid to take her to the hospital, that I might lose her again.

"Numb," she said. "It hurts when I flex."

"Try to hold it up above the level of your heart."

I opened the cab door for her. "Are you coming?"

Pike bounded in. Gloria let go of his leash and followed with far less enthusiasm. I rode in front beside the driver, ankle-deep in KFC boxes full of dry chicken bones.

The ride was swift down side streets of lone walkers, late-shift workers making it home one more time. I tried catching a glimpse of Gloria in the cabbie's rearview mirror and by the streaks of passing headlights and street lamps, but only got a little carsick. He dropped us at the corner of Eleventh. Neither of us mentioned our meeting there.

When we got into my office I sent her straight to the bathroom. The dog went in ahead of her. I brought a chair in from the kitchen and set it before the sink. I started the cold water running. She sat down and put her hand under. As she winced, I saw her face better; it was also burnt, her dark eyebrows singed to sun-baked caterpillars. I soaked a clean washcloth and wrung it out for her to put on her face.

I heard lapping. Pike was drinking from the toilet. I got a pan of water from the kitchen and set it down on the tiled bathroom floor. Pike looked at it like he couldn't imagine what it was for. Gloria called him over. She wiped his face with the washcloth, touching it gently around the eyes and over his singed ears. She started to cry.

While she did that I went out again, downstairs and across the street to the overpriced convenience store. I bought over-priced milk, orange juice, Ritz crackers, cheddar cheese, and dry dog food. It left me fourteen dollars. When I got back, Gloria was still swabbing the dog's scorched chops, but she'd stopped sobbing.

I filled a stainless-steel bowl with dry dog food and cut in chunks of cheddar and mixed them together. I cut thinner slices on a plate, alongside some crackers. My own recipe.

The clang of metal as I set the bowl down on the bathroom floor got both their attentions. I carried the plate over and balanced it on the basin's edge beside Gloria.

"Let me see your hand," I said.

"It's throbbing."

It wasn't as bad as I'd thought. The blisters were pink, not red; thin, not swollen. Maybe only first degree after all.

Pike's snout routed inside the metal bowl licking out the cheese chunks and occasionally crunching down on a hard pellet.

I turned back to Gloria. She was nibbling cheese herself.

I said, "Wednesday night."

"What about it?"

"Wednesday night somebody stole the drugs from the club and you're blamed—"

"This again." She rolled her eyes.

"Later, before dawn Thursday, Ted's killed. There's a connection. Gotta be."

"Teddy wasn't there. I told you, Ellis fired him."

"Even better, he's a spurned lover *and* a disgruntled employee."

"He wasn't my—"

"The point is, by stealing the drugs he jammed up both you and the guys who canned him. It's got his hand all over it."

She opened her mouth and yawned.

"Okay, okay," she said. "But how?"

"Ted was a bartender there. Did he have keys to the club?"

"Yeah, but they took them away."

"He could've made duplicates," I said. "Or only duped those he needed, like the keys to Dee's office. The real question is who he gave them to."

"I don't know. I can't . . . who do you think . . ."

She returned my cold scrutiny with a dreamy, little-girl look. Her eyelids were sack heavy, she only kept them open by wrinkling her forehead higher. Finally they relaxed. The washcloth fell from her fingers into the sink and clogged up the drain. The sink began to fill.

"So? What's the answer, you're so smart?" she asked.

"You told me a friend arranged for you to get a job with Dee. You didn't mean Ted, did you?"

"No way. No, no, Droop said he talked to Ellis. He set it up for me. Droop sorta works there."

"How did you get into the private office?"

"Dunno. I jus' met Droop there. The door was open . . . lights on . . . but nobody . . ."

Her eyes blinked once, then stayed closed.

After a couple of seconds, I reached across and turned the water off. Her eyes shot open, but the lids smoothly unfurled again.

I said, "You can stop soaking it now."

I got out my first-aid kit and removed four large nonstick sterile pads and the adhesive tape. I dried her hand, then put the pads around it, taping them loosely, one over the other.

"That'll hold you," I said. "You can go out and sit down now."

She obeyed my general practitioner's tone, Pike following her out.

I threw away the bandage wrappers and took the washcloth out of the drain. The water swirled down. By the time it was all gone, Gloria was asleep on my couch. Pike curled beneath her on the floor; with his white-and-honey hide, he looked like a bale of wheat.

Exactly what I needed—a crisp-around-the-edges teenage runaway and her orphan pit bull. The worst part, though, was I envied her, some dinky kid from Vermont; three months in the city and people were trying to kill her.

The time was 2:39 A.M. I sat down at my desk and picked up the phone. I called Tigger. Her machine picked up but I didn't leave any message. I hung up and started dialing Matt's number, but stopped myself. Time enough tomorrow to hear I-told-ya-so.

I felt anxious. A sudden, uncontrollable urge in me to go clubbing.

I decided to change first. I changed.

Gloria didn't wake up. Pike snored.

On my way out the front door, I stopped, something bothering me like I was forgetting to turn off the gas. None of the stove burners were on, no water left running. I looked around the apartment, but couldn't think what it was. Then it hit me, it was the apartment itself I was forgetting. I was about to leave it and all it contained in the hands of a girl who the night before stole my watch. *What's wrong with this picture?*

I took one last look at my stereo, my TV, VCR, laptop, fax machine, rack of CDs, and CD player, saying good-bye to them all. My client files were secure in the reinforced-steel safe built into the concrete kitchen floor, also my 9mm Luger, a box of cartridges, and a dozen old love letters from Clair. The really dangerous stuff was locked away.

C H A P T E R

18

When I got into the cab I couldn't remember the address to the club. I felt like I was growing older by the minute, maybe soon to expire. Vaguely, I told the driver, "It's in Chelsea, I think. A nightclub, called the Hell—"

"Twenty-first and Sixth," he said. "Right away, boss."

The cab jerked out into traffic. The driver was a wrinkle-necked, liver-spotted white guy with a salt-and-pepper crew cut you could've cleaned cleats off on, but the music on his radio was earthy reggae, the studio cut of Bob Marley's "Stir It Up."

The strung beads of green traffic lights stretched as far as I could see up Sixth Avenue and stayed *go* for the ten blocks we traveled. Steam churning out of cracks in the road made the air seem like clouded water and the automobiles gliding through it submarines.

On the corner where the driver left me off, a mob of people were gathered, exotically attired in ruffle-collared evening wear and skintight skirts. They were only the end of a line that snaked around the corner and halfway down the block, swollen in spots as if with undigested rats. Three stretch limos—two black, one white—were double-parked up the street where the queue finally terminated outside the entrance to a high, narrow church of time-blackened brown granite.

I went right to the front, to the floodlit entrance shaped like hands held in prayer, and presented myself like I was Somebody. Velvet ropes, strung between waist-high metal stands, delineated the threshold between the red-carpet initiates and those doomed to remain outside all night. Two well-dressed brutes beyond the ropes made the arbitrary decision of who should pass, not a breath of compassion in their stern, muscle-bunched faces.

One of them was Benny, now dressed in an immaculate white suit as if he were there to receive First Communion. A little late. I wished I had a handful of dirt to sling.

He looked bored, listening to a young man squawking about being denied admittance, some skinny white kid wearing John Lennon glasses and a tweed sport coat.

"If you're full, then how come you just let those three in?"

Benny grunted under the strain of communication. "They were in before."

"No, no they weren't, they weren't. I've been here ninety minutes, and they just pulled up in that white limo over there. That one."

Benny turned away and the young man muttered something sharp under his breath. Benny swung back. "What chew call me?"

He unhooked the cordon rope and came through. The kid

started to retreat, backing into the people behind him, stepping on their toes, and getting shoved straight back at Benny.

And I thought that was a *good* time to step in. A fiend for confrontation and I needed my fix.

"Hey, Gentle Ben!" I interceded loudly enough to divert his lunge. "How about getting back to work? I need an usher."

He turned, the fury in his small eyes setting off an equal hatred in mine as I remembered that look from the night before, staring down at me while the boots kept coming in heavy rotation.

"Who the *fuck* are you?" he barked.

I didn't answer.

"Get back in line, asshole."

I didn't obey. Then he placed me.

"Hey, where dafuckuv *you* been? Stosh is up his fucking tree."

"My camp*fire* meeting ran late," I said.

A throwaway line, it duly bounced off his head like a misflung Frisbee. No facial reaction at all to the word *fire*. I wasn't surprised; in that white suit he hadn't been anywhere near Jimmy's shack that night.

Clipped on Benny's belt were his bouncer accessories: a flashlight, keys, Mace, a walkie-talkie, and what looked like a sawed-off cattle prod. He detached the walkie-talkie and spoke into it. A thin black wire ran up into his ear.

"Unit one? This unit four. . . . Stosh? . . . That guy just showed. . . . Uh-huh. . . . Don't know, want me to find out? . . . Uh-huh. . . . Yeah, okay. . . . I'm on it." He clipped the walkie-talkie back on his belt, fiddling with it, adjusting it exactly right.

He called the other bouncer over, a leather-brown Incredible Hulk in green khaki shorts and a black Polo shirt with embroidered red logo.

The second bouncer asked, "Got a problem with this stick, Ben?"

"No, I'm taking him in to Stosh. Cover the door." Then, under his breath. "And keep that weasely geek out."

"Gotcha."

Benny thumbed me to follow. I took a last look down the long line of hapless faces. Still trapped in their limbo of waiting, of wanting, a multitude of eyes watched me as I went in. They were better off where they stood, or so it seemed from my side of the velvet rope.

Benny led me up the stone steps to the door. Written in gilt-edged black letters on red paneling above the arched entry, the warning: ABANDON ALL HYPE YE WHO ENTER HERE.

I asked where he was taking me.

"You'll see."

He gave too much delivery; clearly guile was not his strong suit. Wherever I was going, I wasn't going to like it much.

But why else had I come if not to get beat up in some back room? Somebody had to be punished for setting Jimmy on fire. Maybe it would end up being me.

The giant doors opened, and we passed through into ominous dull thunder.

Within, a fuchsia-haired woman was seated on a barstool checking IDs. She glanced up at Benny and me, then lost all interest. Farther in, on the far side of a pair of standing metal detectors, two tall men frisked new arrivals, looking in purses and turning out pockets searching for concealed weapons and drugs.

One of the men found a small brown vial with a tiny silver spoon attached. He tossed it behind him into a satin-lined collection box, then allowed its owner to pass on unmolested. I wondered where the contraband went at closing.

Benny set off the metal detector as he walked through. He said to the guy stationed there, "Search him."

Long hairy fingers crawled over my body with the swiftness of spider monkeys searching for fleas. They separated me temporarily from my wallet, keys, and crumpled cigarette pack. It's all I had on me, maybe all I had. The man shook his head at Benny.

Benny demanded, "Where is it?"

"I figured you guys would try to burn me, so I took precautions."

It sounded good. I wished it was half true.

"Man, Stosh is going to grind you up," Benny said. "You're one stupid fuck, you know that?"

A fine judge of character. I said, "How's your friend Wade? Still with us?"

He didn't answer, either too busy thinking or else listening to instructions being transmitted over his earpiece. Probably the same thing.

He said, "Come with me."

Through smoothly swinging, wine-dark leather-padded doors, we entered the club proper. A barrage of sound and light battering the senses and sense.

The atmosphere shuddered, charged by multiple dins, pulsating drumbeats, sampled hand-claps, and electronic cries. The thick air's flavor was cigar smoke, cigarettes, pot, clove, and manmade fog being pumped out by a machine high overhead. Laser beams played nimbly through its murk.

The immense dance floor overflowed people. I gazed upon an undulating tract of heads and shoulders, a wave of writhing bodies—so many, I didn't think they could admit so many. What was the room's lawful occupancy, 666? The crowd might've doubled that.

Most of the men were dressed like clean-cut Kennedys cutting loose at the compound, wearing button-down oxfords and khaki slacks. The women displayed more variety, running the gamut from trashy-glitz to international élan, with fretted overlappings. Clubgoers from around the globe, of every shape, size, and language, moved as one people swept up by the melody, flung down by da beat.

At the rear of the church, beneath a yellow-and-orange stained-glass window, where an altar had once stood, was the DJ's control booth. A bare-chested, bald man in polka-dot boxers presided over consoles of turntables and sequencers, spinning round and round as he tweaked knobs, adjusted levels, and sped up the mix.

With one song bleeding profusely into the next, his transfusions permitted his acolytes no rest.

Benny shoved clear a path through the muddle, traversing the muggy arena.

I scanned the expanse of faces lit by a frantic cross-sweep of revolving baby spots. Some were supreme and breathless, others sad and sweaty, a few nasty and utterly lost. All eyes were searching, none happily. It wasn't a place for happiness, only desire.

My roving eyes snagged on a familiar face amid the strangers.

Droopy, dressed in a papery, salmon-colored tracksuit with white-stripe piping. Standing opposite the bar, talking to a tall and slender young woman with long and natty blonde hair wearing a pleated blue skirt and a half-T with the Wonder Bread logo emblazoned across her small uppity chest.

I had to go talk to him. And didn't mind getting a closer look at her.

First I had to lose Benny. It was simple as tying my shoe, I simply ducked down and dodged into the frenzied mob. In a flash I was gone amongst jabbing elbows, bare bellies, and gyrating hip-bones. I'd been in worse places. I didn't look back, just kept low, pushing on in the general direction of the bar, only raising up to get my bearings.

I emerged at the other end of the dance floor, overshooting Droopy by three yards.

He and the girl were still talking—well, shouting; they had to because of the din. As I approached, she was brushing aside his stiff bleached-blonde hair and revealing the exquisite Sacred Heart tattoo on his neck. With her other hand, she slipped something green into the front pocket of his tracksuit. Droopy laughed, brushing the hair back in his eyes, while his other hand neatly zipped up the pocket.

I went to the bar and yelled for Rolling Rock, a vague whimper in the tumult. The glossy bartender, a Morticia Addams lookalike—ebony eyelids and licorice lips—read my lips, pried the cap off a bottle, set it on the bar, and picked up my dropped ten. I waited for change, and waited, and finally decided to get on with my life.

The bottle was cold and dripping ice, the beer quenching and delicious. Leaning against the bar, I gazed back at Droopy over the crest of the bottle. He was down on one knee, apparently tying his shoes, still wearing the same six-layer platform sneakers he'd had on that morning (unless he owned *two* pairs). The longer I looked, the less it looked like he was tying them though; his fingers were instead working farther down along the side of the thick sole. When he stood up again and brushed himself off, he kept one hand cupped in a loose fist.

I pushed from the bar, swam over and sailed by, getting close enough to smell the young woman's fragrance—dewberry and lilacs—and to hear a snatch of what Droopy shouted in her downy-soft ear.

"—run out later, try Fugi's Den when it gets lie—"

It was all I could hear before out of earshot. I took two more steps, stopped, took another long pull off the beer, and looked back at them.

The woman, smiling brightly, tucked something into the elastic waistband of her sky-blue skirt. She blew Droopy a kiss, then twirled off, lithe as a silk streamer. The surrounding throng swallowed her like rolling floodwaters.

Droopy was left all alone. I couldn't have that now, could I?

He didn't hear my hello as I came alongside, so I poked him in the crook of his arm where a hypo would go. No track marks on him though, that wasn't his kick.

His surprise was bland, mellow. He slurred pleasantly, *"Hey, dude, way."*

Even with his big platforms on, he only came to about my height. I got a good whiff of his breath, cherry cough drops over a cloying halitosis.

"Way, Droopy," I said, then shouted, *"R'member me?"*

"Uh . . . *no.*"

"We had lunch together."

I watched his face working, half-hidden by hair. His gray eyes went bleary, troubled by his inability to recall. Gradually though, he accrued some memory.

"Oh yeah, *yeah, you're the* wano wanto weary ware *who glow!*"

I tried making sense of it, but couldn't, so stopped trying and looked around for a quieter place to talk. Ten feet away, a stairwell led down. Down where, I didn't know, but anywhere was better than waiting there for the bouncers to drop down on me.

I grabbed Droopy by the arm and yanked. After my experience with Gloria, I expected some resistance—but he was a man of least. He obeyed with a pleasant, vacuous grin, trotting nimbly along upon his portable stepping stones, unafraid, completely at his ease. As we descended to the lower level, five people on the way up said hello to him, one calling him by another nickname: Rhino.

The staircase ended at the mouth of a narrow warren draped in crimson and pink. We waded into bodies and shoved our way through, jostled every step by hot, alcohol-soaked flesh and sopping shirts. The music was beating too loud to be polite, brute force was necessary to make any headway. I felt like a blood clot in the midst of angina.

Droopy had an easier time, deftly navigating the mired corridor, like he knew its rhythm. He got away from me.

I reached out, but in the confusion got another man's arm. He gave me a warm and inviting smile. I plowed on.

Droopy was five feet away. I fought to keep his bleached-blonde hair in view. But then the corridor turned and he was beyond it. By the time I got there, I couldn't see him.

Several doorways on this stretch opened to side rooms, one the entrance to a huge, dark mosh pit, where skinheads slam-danced to combustible punk rock. Inside, a red-haired girl was puking down the side of a sub-woofer on the floor.

I tried the next room, a cocktail lounge lit in green and blue, glittery sequins dotting aquamarine walls. The bartender was mixing a batch of lime Jell-O shooters. Couples were slow dancing to Babyface. No sign of Droopy.

The crowd grew thinner the farther I moved along the corridor. Finally, I reached a section of the passage where only five giggling people stood smoking pot in a hollowed-out, blunt-tipped cigar. Beyond them was a doorway fringed in gold paint. Inside the music was soft and abstract like a pod of humpbacks reciting haiku to ABBA instrumentals.

The room was shaped like Florida laid on its western shore, and was as dense and shadowy as the Everglades. From the low ceiling, dust-heavy festoons of streamers hung like Spanish moss. There were private retro-diner booths built into each wall. I made a circuit, poking my head into each one until I found Droopy sitting alone in a curtained booth down by the Keys.

A napkin up to his face: I thought at first he was blowing his nose, but he kept backing up his shoulders as if inhaling. He was. The vapors in the booth were palpable. *Ether.* It was okay with me. I wanted him a little gaga when we spoke. Maybe it'd have the same effect as Pentothal. I shoved into the seat beside, penning him in.

Droopy dropped the napkin to his lap. Glass nicked the table.

All innocence, he said, "Hey, man, where'd you go? Thought I lost you."

"Sure, whatever. Where's your friend Seth tonight?"

"He's here. Left him upstairs. Hey, you wanna talk to him?" He started sliding across toward me. "I can—"

"No. Let's sit a while, get familiar. We hardly got to talk this morning. By the way, let me compliment you. That's a pretty clever dodge you work."

"Huh?"

"You know. The thing with your shoe. I bet it fools them at every door you're frisked."

Even with his head swaddled in vapors, he bolted upright in the

seat. Probably he'd developed a tolerance by now anyway, so it
took more and more of the stuff to give him the buzz he remembered and craved.

Not so me. The ether wobbled my vision so I had to lean out of
the booth for a gulp of fresh air.

Droopy said, "Huh?"

I said, "Your craftsmanship and ingenuity are truly laudable."
The fumes had really got to me. "Mind if I take a look at them?"

The request was only magician's patter as I ducked below the
table and grabbed his bulky left shoe off the floor. I got both my
hands on it and yanked up. He slid down in the seat, tried to pull
back, but I held on tight. I struggled to pry off the platform
sneaker. Undoing the top lace, I finally wrenched the sockless
heel free and his foot slipped out. His toenails were varnished tan-
gerine. I resurfaced holding the big shoe.

"Whew! Ever hear of Odor-Eaters?"

"What the hell you think you doin'?! Give me my fuckin' shoe
back!"

"In a minute."

I turned it over in my hand, scanning the creases between the
stacks until I found the spot: the clenched teeth of a zipper running along the insole. I grabbed the tab and dragged it across.

Droopy tried stopping me, clawing his fingers down my arm,
raking his nails into my skin. I'd had enough abuse for one day.
Adhering to the trickle-down theory of violence, I jabbed my left
elbow into his chest, the neighborhood of his solar plexus. He
collapsed, choking, into the far corner of the booth.

Shaking the tingle from my funny bone, I got back to unzip-
ping the shoe. It revealed a hollow sole between the layers of
spongy foam rubber, a secret compartment as wide and deep as
an open billfold, only it didn't have money inside.

I emptied the contents out onto the starburst-linoleum tabletop.
Like picking up a carcass and watching the maggots spill out:
hundreds of yellow mini baggies cascaded down in a flurry.

I don't know what I expected, but being right for a change was low on the list. It took a minute to sink in. I picked up one of the baggies with just a fingertip, the plastic clinging to my skin oil. It was packed with a quarter-teaspoon of fine white powder. I held it in front of my nose and examined the faint blue impression of a curved horn.

Droopy regained control of his breathing, enough to mutter a hurt and angry: "What's your fuckin' problem?"

His eyes were wide and alert as he massaged the sore spot where I'd elbowed him. The pain had jarred him back to our unglamorous world of hard realities. An anxiety tic snagged his cheek like cold skin on a pudding.

I raked all the tiny packets into a pile in front of me.

"You really expected to make a killing tonight, look at this. Or were you just afraid to leave it behind in the dorm?"

The seriousness of the situation was dawning on him; I could actually track his growing unease in the twist and turn of his mouth. I decided to hit him with everything I had and see what happened.

"You were Ted's inside man, the one he gave his keys to. This is the shit you stole from Ellis Dee's office Wednesday night, right before you set up Gloria."

His color drained encouragingly—encouraging to me.

"You took a lot of risks for this, but Ted got most of the reward. He got revenge on his girl *and* his boss. What was in it for you?"

Droopy said angrily, "Ted said he had a buyer lined up, goin' pay us fifty grand for it, like twenty times what it's worth. Couldn't fucking believe it." He winced, reliving the loss and frustration of the fantasy. "But it was all bullshit."

"Then what, he tried to stiff you?"

"No, cuz by then I wanted to give it back. See . . . I mean, I talked to Seth and he showed me how Ted had to be bullshitting, he didn't have no buyer. He was right, too. All this shit and no—"

Salvation flickered in his dismal gray eyes. He blurted, "Hey, guy, look . . . I'll split it with you! No, really."

"No, thanks," I said. "I've seen how your splits come out. I think you killed Ted."

The leap terrified him, he didn't want to take it with me. He shook his head against it, but pretense was out of reach. He didn't even have the sense to act surprised about Ted's death.

Finding his voice again, he meekly offered, "Take it *all*, man. Take it."

I felt a little sick to my stomach, not only from the fumes in the booth, but they weren't helping either. It was way past time for police involvement; I'd already delayed too long dropping myself down that dark pit. But at least now I had something resembling evidence to hand them, and a suspect other than Gloria to look at. They could sort out the rest. All I had to do now was get Droopy to them.

I started scooping up the packets of Rhino and dropping them inside the shoe, shoving them down into the toe.

I told Droopy he better take off his other shoe unless he wanted to limp out.

"Where'm I going?"

"With me. I'm making a citizen's arrest. Kinda corny, I know, but it's late."

"I'm not—"

"Listen, dweeb, you're walking or I'm lugging you. I'm sure this place is used to seeing people get carted out unconscious, so it won't even cause a ripple. What's it going to be?"

He massaged the sore spot where I had elbowed him, recalling it like it was only yesterday. That should've tipped me. But then, he obediently turned in his seat, crooked his knee, and began undoing the other shoe's lace.

I finished collecting evidence and started to slide out of the booth.

I didn't think he could move so quickly—desperation, I suppose.
I expected some fight out of him, but not the sudden white flash
that blinded me. Even before I knew what to grab at, the cloth was
over my nose and mouth, and sudden chill—sharp as alcohol,
cold as liquid nitrogen—splashed my cheeks. I tightened my lips
against its sickening-sweet vapor. Ether . . . *Ethhhhhhhhhher*.

Like drowning in polar waters, the ice flow gushed up my nose
and down my throat, heavier than air, colder than extreme despair.
I gagged on it—and breathed it back fuller, deeply inhaling it.

I couldn't break his hold, couldn't reach him from behind.

Mist encroached round my edges and I wondered from where it
came. The booth pitched and lurched like a rickety carnival ride
snapping its last linchpin. My head felt extremely small—tiny
even—yet somehow of far more significance, like the last daisy
petal left to pluck to decide, once and for all, "Love me? Love me
not?"

I still had his big platform shoe in my hand. With a final effort,
I blindly flung it over my shoulder. My reward was a soft thud and
a loosening of Droopy's sticky hold.

I fell forward out of the booth, hands up to cushion my impact
with the floor. But someone moved it on me, so that I only fell farther, down straight through the foundation, like a spirit walking
through walls, gravity's unrelenting yearning drawing me down,
immersing me in the black earth below Manhattan.

CHAPTER 19

Thunder clapped and woke me. I melted back, repoured into my mold, and became solid again, the left side of my face sting-tingling. Disoriented: my last clearest recollection was of lying down at seven P.M. The rest was a chunky blur of evening. Maybe when the eyes came up again, I'd still be on my couch, and find the less distinct memories of Gloria's phone call, Jimmy getting torched, and my spiral down the Hellhole were only stale leftovers of tacky nightmare.

Then another clap of thunder rocked my head and this time I recognized the slap.

A man's voice, deep and modulated as late-night radio, said, "Thank you, that's enough. He's up now."

My eyes opened crisscrossed and wouldn't align. I blinked a few times, it didn't help. I shook my head to see what that would do, and felt regret.

There wasn't enough room in my head for all the pain lodged there; I'd overbooked again, much of it doubling-up in my temples and tearing out the permanent fixtures. I held my head very still and opened my eyes again. Things were clearer.

The room was long and narrow and high-ceilinged; it was like waking up at the bottom of a cereal box. I saw neither window nor door. The four walls were paneled in marble-veined mirrors, opposing reflections curling into infinity. Beneath my feet I felt more than heard the smothered groans of the active dance club going on.

I was in an upper room of the renovated church, then, and seated in a beautiful antique leather club chair built of lustrous, silken-smooth mahogany. The leather was black morocco (what wallets are made of), edged in burnished brass tacks. To my right stood a silver art deco ashtray shaped like a greyhound. To my left loomed Stosh, shaped like a dilapidated windmill, the open palm of his right hand held down by his side, ready in case I needed another restorative slap. Or for any reason.

Overhead, four clear Plexiglas propellers fanned the air at varied speeds; one slower than the rest revolved counterclockwise. I got vertigo.

Directly in front of me was a wide, rounded black desk, curved like the capital letter *C*. All onyx, like a still pool of premium motor oil, not so much as a telephone, a paper clip, or a speck of dust upon it. The man seated at its center was Ellis Dee, his gaunt, egret face hanging by the points of two stabbing blue eyes. Wide lips pursed, cheeks raw-boned, jaw slightly moving, he seemed to be perpetually mincing a chewed-off hangnail.

"Welcome back," he said, tight-lipped.

"What time is it?"

"A touch after four."

I spit a curse. Cursing hurt my head. I reached up and touched a tender deformity cunningly tucked beneath my brow. The point of impact with floor.

Ellis Dee said, "Yes, a bad time, four A.M. I've never cared for it myself, an ugly hour. You might want to take some deep breaths."

I took his suggestion and the breaths. Any port in a storm. After a few deep ones, I said, "You're Ellis Dee."

He nodded. "I am. And you're Payton Sherwood. You were searched while you were out."

"How considerate."

"Expedient to learn you're not wearing a wire and we can speak freely. You're a private investigator. Why did you come here?"

"I had an appointment."

"But you haven't come prepared. Who are you working for, Mr. Sherwood?"

"Gloria Manlow. I'm her go-between."

"You're going to return what she stole from us?"

"No, that's impossible," I said. "She never took it. But it doesn't matter. You don't want it back now anyway, Mr. Diecklicht."

He had no reaction to my using his real name. Maybe I pronounced it wrong. (Lord knows I tried to.)

"Don't I?" he said, precisely spitting the words.

"It's all gone bad. Been tainted. It's already contributed to three deaths."

"Who told you that?" He was offended. "That's ridiculous. It's a perfectly harmless substance. It's been researched."

"Maybe when taken internally. It's the external effects that are killing people."

"What extern—"

"Your boy Stosh here for one. He caused a death today trying to recover it."

"Shut your—"

Ellis spoke over Stosh's objections.

"Yes, yes, an unfortunate accident. Stosh informed me. I even spoke to the police earlier. They're charging Wade with manslaughter in Orloff's death. A moot point since he's on the critical list, and his prognosis isn't good."

"But you're keeping fingers crossed," I said.

"The point is, as far as the police are concerned the case is closed. They think it was a *crime passionel*. Wade went looking for his girlfriend—Gloria—and matters got out of hand. I'm not responsible for the love lives of my staff. So why don't we stop fencing and get back to why you came here tonight. Your money is here." He patted a breast pocket, a hollow rum-pum-pum. "A thousand dollars, correct?"

"I told you I don't have your stuff. I never did."

Stosh growled, "Then that bitch's still got it."

"You've been chasing your tail," I said. "Gloria never took it. Someone else did."

"I *know* she took it."

"Which shows you *know* shit."

Ellis cleared his throat.

"Let's not dissemble. If you never had it, what are these? They were found in the booth where you were collapsed." He pulled out an envelope and emptied it on the black desk. A couple dozen packets of the Rhino hovered on top. "These are the same as those which were stolen."

"I know," I said. "I got them from the thief."

"Who?"

"This kid called Droopy. You must know him."

Stosh farted out his mouth. "No fucking way, man! Now I *know* you're bullshit."

"How's that?"

"Droopy didn't take it. You think I didn't think of that weasel? When I saw it gone, I nabbed him right away. I found him on the dance floor, strip-searched him right there. He was clean. The only other person up here that night was that bitch."

"Droopy took it, all right," I said, "and hid it on himself where you'd never think to look."

"I made him drop his—"

"I said where you *wouldn't* think to look—his platform shoes. They've got a zippered compartment in the side."

Dee said, "I remember he mentioned once . . . but no, I can't see Droopy doing this. We treat him too well here, like a prince. He comes and goes as he pleases, never pays a cent. Why would he spoil that by stealing something we normally give him gratis?"

"He's prone to suggestion, malleable-minded. I think he was sold the idea by another of your employees, Ted Wylie."

Ellis brushed my suggestion aside. "Theodore Wylie is no longer employed here."

"Or anywhere."

"He was fired two days before the theft. He didn't take it."

"I think he made dupes of your keys and convinced Droopy to use them to break in here and rip you off. Ted wanted to get back at you and his girlfriend for dumping him. Why did you fire him anyway?"

"Bad manners, but that's not important."

"Everything is, in murder."

"I already explained to you about Wade."

"I mean Ted's murder. Didn't Stosh tell you?"

Dee turned steel-dagger eyes onto Stosh's face and left them shining there.

Stosh said, "I don't know what the fuck he's talking about."

Ellis Dee's gaze glazed. "Stosh, could you give us a few minutes alone?"

"Ellis, no way."

"Please, I believe I can conclude this quicker myself. You two seem to have a mutual antagonism that keeps dragging us off the point. Please, won't you?"

"Don't listen to him. I didn't kill Ted. Why would I?"

"I know, I know. Don't worry. I'm going to explain that to him. Okay?"

Stosh grumbled dissent, but did as he was told. He shuddered the flooring stamping out, but the door shut behind him with a soft click not a slam.

Ellis stood and walked out from behind his desk. He was over six feet tall and built like a wind chime, arms and legs, long and dangly. He sat on the edge of his circular desk, crossing his legs, knee-upon-bony-knee.

"Payton, this has gotten out of hand. Try to understand: When I first told Stosh to seek recovery, I had no idea of the scope it would take. I spoke in heat, upset by my desk being ransacked. I never lock it, you see. I trust my people."

"Maybe you shouldn't. They've been doing bad things on your behalf."

"Well, given the dimensions of my operation, the number of people I employ, the latitude I have to give them—well, naturally, some may act rashly of their own initiative. Neither with my knowledge nor my consent. Usually I encourage this."

"But in this instance, three men are dead."

"Three?"

"A homeless man killed tonight. Set on fire between midnight and one."

"A homeless—what's that to do . . . ? You can't be serious."

"He witnessed Ted's murder."

"And since you think Stosh killed Ted, you think he's responsible for this, too?"

"Or you."

"Ridiculous. He's been here since we opened at ten. The staff can confirm that."

"I'm sure they will, but that's not important; it could've been subcontracted."

"It's laughable Stosh would commit *murder* over a few thousand dollars. I know the man."

"How much money *would* it take?"

"That's always the final question, isn't it?"

Ellis Dee drew a long breath and stretched out his legs, then crossed them like pruning shears. "The bottom line is, I prefer that my establishment be kept out of this altogether. It's not the law so much as the press. If what you say about Ted is true, coming so soon on top of Wade's accident, it would cause unwanted publicity. So since it's getting late, I'll ask *you*: How much?"

I did the math, rounded up to the nearest thousand and settled on nine thousand dollars: I would just about break even and could start over with a clean credit slate. So little to make me happy. Nice to think about, and it wasn't my *scruples* that stopped me either. It was Dee that put me off. I don't mind indulging powerful people with the illusion they can buy anything and anyone, but it would be a disservice to Dee. After all the buildup, he was nothing but another flake playing with power, well on his way to devising his own horrible end.

He didn't need my kind of help.

"It is late," I said, "so I'll settle for everybody gets nothing. How's that sound to you?"

"Too good," he said suspiciously. "Are you sure?"

"Yeah, I'm sure. As long as you stay clear of Gloria, I'm not interested. But you might think about getting a choke chain for Stosh."

"Agreed. I've no hard feelings against Gloria. I'd hoped she knew that. I love the kids. When this all first happened, if she'd only come and talked to me—well, none of *this* would be happening, we wouldn't be here talking now."

"Sounds lovely, a dream to make come true."

I stood too quickly and felt woozy. Turning wide, I overspun,

and braced myself on the chair. I couldn't see a door. Nothing behind me but *me*, reflected in more mirrors.

Ellis stood erect. He curled a long finger.

"Come this way, you can leave by the back."

He motioned me to the other side of his desk and walked to a
far corner of the room, where he faced a Janus reflection of himself in the mirrored panels. He placed his right hand flat against
one panel and pushed. The pressure sprung an inner touch latch,
the panel swinging free, out and open.

It revealed the head of a wooden staircase going down. The
narrowness and tilt of the warped boards reminded me of the
basement steps in my grandmother's house. They smelled the same,
too, like the dust-lather on Mason jars full of ancient, forgotten
preserves. Pickled cauliflower, beet jelly, turnip jam; all delicacies
in the old country.

"This lets you out on Twentieth Street," he said, "behind the
club. Uh, you might want to use the handrail going down."

I looked in to make sure the stairs went all the way down before I took the first step past tattered party decorations stored
from last year's Valentine's Day, Halloween, and New Year's Eve.
After another step, it occurred to me that this back way could've
been used by either Stosh or Ellis Dee to leave the building without any of the staff knowing. That's when the lights went out as
the door above me snicked seamlessly shut.

"Hey!"

I stood in darkness waiting for light to return, just me and my
heart (I'd forgotten what a powerful companion it could be) beating against my lung like a soft leather tom-tom. Not a hairline of
light revealed itself. Gripping the handrail, I took a step down into
formless black.

Lighting a match would've left me more than blind with a
superimposed, phantom orange dot in front of my face when
the match went out, so I didn't bother, just continued down in
darkness.

Satin-and-lace hearts hanging loosely from the wall brushed dust off onto my face.

When I came to the bottom step, I didn't know it at first and tried to take another, my foot slapping prematurely on cement foundation.

Groping my way along the brick wall, I came to the edge of a passage and followed it. A weak red glow floated ahead in the distance. Working closer, tripping over dry mops and empty plastic drums, I made out the red letters: x, i, and t. The bulb below the e burnt out.

I pumped the exit's panic bar and fresh air eddied in, scented with springtime. Not alone a fragrance, but a temperature, too, and a motion. Emotion.

Through a side-alley door, I reemerged into the nighttime world of Manhattan, bright with street lamp novas and comet clusters of shooting headlights. Only the sky above was dark—a dull purple like the bald patches on old black velvet—its universe of stars faded by the city's glare.

I smoked my last cigarette. Feeling distinctly like I knew less than I did before, as if along the way I'd lost information somehow, not found out anything. All in all, it was a big disappointment.

But in that way at least, no different from any other night I'd gone out clubbing.

CHAPTER 20

I stopped in at an all-night doughnut shop off
Union Square for coffee. Four forty-two A.M. I
wasn't the only customer. Five teenagers,
dressed to shock, were noshing bagels and spinning on the stools. One girl had pink plastic see-
through pants and clown-orange hair braided
with tiny white seashells. She was wearing a
white T-shirt with the light gray letters CK on the
back and FU on the front.

The Saturday morning papers were out, I
bought one of each and started scanning. Nothing in the *Times* reflected the New York I'd been
negotiating, so I tried the others. On page seventeen of the *News* was a paragraph on Powers
Orloff. Police reported the Brooklyn artist's
death was the result of a domestic dispute involv-

ing the ex-boyfriend of one of his underage models (name with-held). The assailant in custody, Wade Schmidt, twenty-two, also injured in the fall, remained hospitalized in a coma.

Nothing about Orloff in the *Post*, but on page thirty-eight—so small I missed it on the first pass—three uncaptioned lines of filler below a carpet sale ad reported:

The decomposing body of a man, discovered by neighbors in his Lower East Side apartment Friday afternoon, is being ruled a suicide by police. Theodore Wylie, 27, was found with a plastic bag knotted around his head and neck.

Just one reason I never believe what I read in the papers.

Not an epitaph you'd wish on your worst friend, but at least Ted had made it into print. I knew Jimmy's death wouldn't rate ink. Even if it did, what could they possibly write: HOMELESS JUNKIE SETS SELF ON FIRE?

I tore out both articles and left the rest folded up in the booth. I paid my check.

At the register, the kids were anteing up their dollars and cents for the bill.

The girl with shells in her clown-orange hair was goading, "Come on, there's plenty places left to go."

Her voice was so vibrant, so clear, I turned to see how her bleary-eyed friends were responding. Some of her energy trans-mitted. They raised their heads higher; one asked, "Where?"

"Save the Robots, or that after-hours down Ludlow or Orchard?"

"We don't have enough for cab fare," one whined.

"We'll walk . . . Come on. It's early."

I couldn't remember ever having that much energy. Almost five by the Con Ed clock presiding over Fourteenth Street. The pre-dawn sky was fading to a stonewashed denim blue.

The thought of blue jeans made me think of Jimmy, dressed in denim from head to toe. I kept on thinking about him and how his death would be swept under the carpet like the other two. Not because of "conspiracy" or because "people didn't care," but because no one knew enough about him to care, and now never would have a chance. And Jimmy wouldn't have his "another second chance."

I walked home with my hands in my pockets, too tired to carry them.

When I got to the corner and looked up at my arched windows, no lights were on. She was probably still sleeping. If I walked in now, I'd wake her. Or the dog would.

I kept going with no idea where. At first, simply east.

Not enough money left to buy a pack of cigarettes, I told myself I didn't want a cigarette, didn't need one. Just like the government's plan to get kids to quit smoking.

I walked by the Asher Levy schoolyard on East Eleventh. The concrete playground was closed, but not empty. Four people were camping out under the jungle gym, huddled together beneath one large gray-stained comforter, their black combat boots poking out the bottom. I heard two separate snores.

At First Avenue, the only traffic was two garbage trucks spitting black smoke in a wild race uptown toward Twenty-third Street. I cut across. I knew where I was headed now, back to Jimmy's. Maybe too late to learn about his life, but I could still learn *from* his death.

At that hour Alphabet City is a no-man's-land no one should walk idly, but I wasn't idle; I moved through the dismal surround with that shield of determination equally adorning the possessed and the plain crazy.

The eastern sky blushed a peach-orange from the steady advance of dawn.

In front of Jimmy's, the sidewalk was piled waist-high with burnt plywood and two-by-fours, and an assortment of charred wreckage, the remains of a life lived on the street.

Something else, too. Four white devotional candles arranged in a shrine, their orange-yellow flames burning low, and three cut yellow roses, the petals brown round the edges and beaded with crystal morning dew. Beneath them, sheets of paper fluttered in the wind. I knelt down to look at one, and read:

Dear Jimmy,

I didn't know you enough to talk to you. But when I first came here you were one of the first people I met. You used to tell stories or read your poems in the park. You were always stressing the positive. I'm sorry we never got to talk. I'll miss you.

Love, Nancy

I didn't read the others, none addressed to me.

Aside from the letters was a half-pint of vodka, a full roach clip, a torn half of a one-dollar bill, five quarters, a broken-spine copy of *Franny and Zooey*, and a Snickers bar. Items to take with you on a long trip. I wished I'd had something meaningful to contribute.

The gate to the lot was open, the motorcycle chain unlocked and hanging from the same place Jimmy had put it that afternoon.

I followed the muddy path to the fire-gutted shack. The garden about lay in ruins, bootprints through every plot of earth. Plants lay crushed, in shambles. The cucumbers and tomatoes were reduced to vegetable matter.

On the spot where Jimmy's home had stood, a bonfire mound and burnt black earth. The odor of wetted ashes was strong.

Much of the debris had been cleared by the firemen the night before to prevent a flare-up. They'd dragged free the caved-in ceiling and the right side wall, which had collapsed atop Jimmy.

The front wall had fallen outward, in one solid piece, buckling under the weight of the roof. Its surface was covered in muddy tracks, but the wood had hardly burned at all. Most of the fire then had been concentrated at the rear of the shack.

I walked across the fallen wall and started picking my way through the rubble. I cleared trash, flinging away a lawn chair frame, some burnt planks, and a solid mass of melted rubber, plastic, and wire that might've been his radio–cassette player.

I couldn't find his kerosene heater, probably carted away as evidence or simply for disposal. On the ground, I followed the scorched white pour-patterns left by the kerosene's spread. The trail led from the center of the room to the right-hand corner and an unburnt patch of carpeting in the shape of an S. The spot where Jimmy died, curled in on himself, his body protecting the underlying carpet from flames.

Which meant he'd been lying there before it started, and had never moved again. Either dead or unconscious. Maybe knocked out and left for the fire to do the dirty work. They sometimes call arson the poor man's gun. If so, this one had come cheaper than most: Jimmy provided his own accelerant.

Looking for traces of blood on the unscorched carpet, I found none. But there are plenty of ways to knock out a man without leaving visible traces, I knew that from experience, still tasting the cloying sweetness of ether in my lungs.

I searched around in the clutter until I found what remained of Jimmy's footlocker. The lid was open and the papers inside re-duced to ashes. My hands fished around until they felt something hard, smooth, and dangerously sharp. The hunting knife Jimmy had pulled on me. I grasped the flat of its blade and carefully pulled it out, not cutting myself. Go figure. The imitation-bone handle had melted and turned brown. The silvery blade now had a dull, splotchy blue-black sheen.

I wrapped the knife in a tattered rag and dropped it in my jacket pocket.

One of Jimmy's sketch pads and several of his books hadn't been consumed by the flames, merely burned crumbling around all the edges. I picked up *The Complete Poems of Emily Dickin-son*. Soggy with ashwater, it fell open where the spine was

cracked, to poem No. 135, which Jimmy had quoted me the first
line of: "Water, is taught by thirst."

> *Land—by the Oceans passed.*
> *Transport—by throe—*
> *Peace—by its battles told—*
> *Love, by Memorial Mold—*
> *Birds, by the Snow.*

I tore it out and kept it, but not because it told me what had
happened to Jimmy.

I tried to flip through the sketch pad's pages; they clung damp
together. I worked my fingernails between and turned them one
by one. Most were blank. I counted six complete drawings in all.
Two were sketches of men hefting barbells; three, studies of a
woman, topless, sitting on the edge of a chair with her eyes shut.
The last drawing was of a pair of faces, eyeless, with the caption
Two Martians Watching Their Murder.

I stared into their blank, shared impassivity a long time,
until through the clumsy caricature I recognized the faces, knew
them both.

I put the pad someplace to dry, then went back to sifting
through more ashes, not sure what I was looking for, only seeing
what I could find.

After fifteen minutes of clawing the cinders, broken glass,
rusted nails, and melted-plastic lumps, my fingers closed around
something oddly shaped like the Playboy Bunny logo. I brushed it
off. A glob of melted nylon with two blackened keys sticking out
in a V. Jimmy's keys. One to the motorcycle chain lock on the
front gate. The other key, smaller, belonging to the padlock on
the shack's front door.

I needed to see the front door. I tried to lift the fallen wall, but
couldn't, too heavy for me to raise alone. But I was alone.

I scouted around the yard and found two strong wooden

boards, one long, one short, and carried them over. Then I got a couple of garden gnomes to help me.

I set one of the statues down on its side in front of the wall and laid the board across it seesaw, making a lever with the plaster gnome as my fulcrum. I fitted the board under the wall and pushed down on the other end, prying the wall up off the ground.

When I'd gotten it up two feet high, I propped the second gnome under it, and balanced the wall's weight on his pointy head. His face was missing.

There was enough space now to wedge the shorter board under it. I propped up the wall so it looked like a giant rabbit trap, then I took the longer board, braced, and kicked it under. I strained to raise the lean-to higher, higher, splinters digging deep into palms. Grunting, I pushed the wall back, and with all my strength heaved it over. For one moment, the facade stood balanced on end, then it fell away and toppled.

I jumped clear. The crash resounded in the isolated lot like a cannon blast. The stillness of early morning was only briefly disturbed. When the ash and dirt settled, I walked to the upturned wall and looked down at it. The front door's hasp was strapped across, and on its loop, the steel padlock was locked in place.

Whoever had set the fire had locked Jimmy inside the shack to ensure success.

I cleaned off the padlock key and inserted it in the lock. I turned the key.

The steel body dropped down, dangling on its shackle. The padlock swung out left, telling me what I wanted to know.

CHAPTER 21

I felt like I was running out of time, and at the same time stepping outside of its bounds, stopping the clock. Any second the paradox was going to spit me out and swallow me whole. I straddled the moment, concentrating on getting where I was going.

The Fugitive's Den was on Orchard Street, a block south of Houston and one west of Ludlow. I walked the mile or so from Jimmy's shack, thinking everything through, taking long strides with the objects in my pockets slamming against me, a constant reminder of the weight of things.

That narrow tract of Orchard was home to bricked-up tenements, occupied only at street level by wholesale and retail fabric stores, all closed up tight behind their graffiti-scrawled roll-down gates, barricaded against the regular storm of night.

The after-hours club had the only visible traces of life at that hour, a lit awning and a wide-open door. No one was standing outside, or inside when I first stepped in.

Dusty and cluttered, it looked like an abandoned renovation. A few stools, covered in drop cloths, and six large stucco urns were all grouped to one side. On the opposite side were stacked sawhorses and plywood, sawdust piles and anthills of nails.

The creaky floorboards were time-soiled, blackened slats. The old-fashioned tin-paneled ceilings were pressed in a flower pattern. Both details remnants of the building's history, when the neighborhood around it teemed with thousands of new immigrants, and the store was maybe a kosher deli or Chinese laundry. Nothing but a dead end now.

"It's downstairs," a light voice rose up.

A young woman's face appeared above and beyond the rims of urns. It was the same girl I'd seen in the doughnut shop, the one with the seashells in her hair.

She stepped out and revealed a wall-mounted pay phone behind her.

"The doorman'll be right back," she said. "He's peeing. But you can go in."

"Thanks." Only there didn't seem to be a place *to* go in. I didn't see stairs.

She tilted her head as she moved in closer, her seashells bumping into each other, tinkling. She asked, "Do I know you?"

"No."

"But I—hey, wait, you were at that doughnut dump."

"Yeah." I laughed. "That's right."

"Did you follow me here?" Her eyes glistened at the prospect I was stalking her.

"No," I said. "It's just a coincidence, I'm afraid."

She shook her head, seashells riling a tempest. Firmly she said, "I don't believe in coincidences."

"You should, they're all you're ever going to get."

"I mean, I do but, *I* think we're all like . . . in a computer. The circuits, you know, switching, like dominoes falling over. One triggers another triggers another triggers a—"

"I get it. A chain reaction."

"Yeah, so then all this stuff starts happening. And there really is, like, a *design*, only we never get to see it. See? Because we're . . . we're those people in the bleachers at football games who hold up colored cards to spell out words *they* never get to read."

Maybe she had something there. Giganto-Vision stadium TV screens aside.

"I still didn't follow you," I told her. "I overheard a friend say he'd be here. Wherever here is."

"Too bad."

She got over it. Her friends showed then, emerging at the back from behind a dark velvet curtain that had concealed a wrought-iron spiral staircase leading down.

Passing beyond the heavy drape, I met a cool, damp, and smoky atmosphere, and descended corkscrew into the fog.

The low-ceilinged space was a firetrap, but exceptionally homey. Except for the flickering fluorescent over the bar, the place was illuminated solely by shotglass-candles distributed unevenly around the room, and elsewhere creating fat patches of no light.

A couple dozen people were inside, some seated at tables and others in sagging armchairs or on split-seat sofas surrounded by coffee tables and nightstands.

I looked toward the shadows in the back and found Seth and Droopy seated at a café table with a cold, snuffed-out candle between them. On the way over I picked up a lit one from another table and carried it with me. The hot glass seared my fingers and I dropped it quickly on their table. It skidded across, chinking against the dead one.

"Cheers," I said.

Their young faces shone ghastly in the yellow shimmer. Seth shrank from it and looked up. Droopy only slouched lower in his seat and gazed on at the candle flame in tranquil fascination. His smile beatific, but its batteries running low.

For better lighting, I leaned in, letting the candle lightly toast my chin. Seth saw me clearly. His hands dry-squeegeed across the tabletop and rested clamped on its edge.

"What are you doing here?"

"Like you said this morning, the city's strands converge like a spiderweb."

I dragged a chair over and sat down. We made a triangle.

"You don't mind if I join," I said. "Long day. You understand."

Droopy slung his head round and focused on me as though through layers of fruit basket cellophane. Grinning, his rubbery lips made a deflating balloon noise.

"Hey, heeey, whadaya get lost, man? Seth wuz sayin' he wooden be s'prized if—"

Seth's chair scraped, he stood up. "Come on, we're leaving."

Droopy's face screwed up in consternation. He said, "No, I got hang. Expecting people to show. Gotta really hang."

I said pleasantly, "Sit down, Seth. We're friends here. No hard feelings, if that's your worry. I'm not here to start trouble. Actually, hoping to end some. Let's talk."

Unconvinced, but he reclaimed his seat, and his grip on the table.

"I've nothing to say to you," he said. The melodrama seemed to fortify him, stiffen his backbone. "You can talk all you want, but we're not saying a single word."

The last bit directed at Droopy, who smiled, glad to be included. He made a visible effort to pay closer attention.

"That's fine," I said. "You just listen to my voice then. I've interesting things to tell you. Unless you'd rather read about it in the papers?"

"*Things?* What things?"

"They found Ted's body. Took them long enough, huh? Still it must be a relief, I mean, I know how these details can play nasty tricks on your mind after a while. You catch yourself talking in the past tense about him when no one else knows he's dead."

"I never—" Seth stopped himself. He let go of the table and held his thumbs inside balled fists. "What are you talking about?"

"You two murdered Ted."

"You're out of your mind."

"It doesn't change the fact."

"I'm not going to listen to—"

"Sit, you'll miss the best part. See, I don't give a shit you killed him. You could kill him again for all I care. That's not what this is about."

My words penetrated Droopy's dazed confusion and ignited an active response. "Hey, maaaan, we didn't fucking kill him. That's bullshit. Tell him, Seth, tell him how it was. Ted's own goddamn fault. He shouldna tried to—"

Seth went ballistic, off-the-monitor.

"Shut your *fucking* mouth! Now!"

"What's the matter? It was all in self-de—"

Seth bashed his left fist down on the table. The candles jostled and jittered, the lit one sloshing molten wax, threatening darkness, then righting itself, revived fire.

The pyrotechnics startled Droopy. I urged my chair closer to him.

"Self-defense, huh? That's kind of a hard sell, don't you think? Especially when you tied a bag around his head? But I guess you could always claim future threat. That how Seth sold you on it Thursday morning? I mean, you had an argument, right? With Ted, and what? Gave him a good tap? But *you* never meant to kill him, did you, huh, Droopy?"

"No way. But Seth freaked, said we had to *finish* it. I didna know."

I looked over at Seth, his eyes picking apart my face like dissection needles.

"Relax," I said. "Like I told you before, I don't care about Ted. And get this, no one does. Not even the cops. They care so little they're labeling it suicide."

Seth's composure slipped away. "What?"

For the first and only time then, I saw his real face. He looked so young, lost. I wondered briefly if I was doing the right thing. Enough time to worry about that later.

I took out the item on Ted I'd torn out, handed it to him.

Seth held it between both hands, a slip of paper as big as the fortune in a fortune cookie. He read it, I don't know how many times, but enough to have memorized it.

I snatched it back and said, "Page thirty-eight of the *Post*. Buy your own copy."

I gave it to Droopy to read. But it was asking too much, his attention lagged before the second syllable. He said, "So what, what's that mean? We're in the *clear*?"

"No," I said. " 'Fraid not, Droopy. You see, it's a lot like the club scene. The illusion only works so long as everyone believes. An anonymous phone call to the cops and I could bring up all the ugly houselights like"—*snap*—"that."

Droopy's eyes bulged. For the first time, he looked worried. I guess couching it in terms he understood finally drove home the seriousness.

Seth said, "Don't listen to him, Droopy, he's bluffing us. It's a suicide, the article says so. He doesn't have proof otherwise or he wouldn't be here trying to get *us* to talk."

"I don't need proof, jerk. There was a witness."

Seth asked, "Who? What witness? Witness to what?"

I took a soggy sheet of paper out of my pocket, unfolded it, and

revealed its black burnt edges. I flopped it down on the table beside the candle. It was the sketch from the drawing pad, the one
captioned *Two Martians Watching Their Murder*.

"What's that?"

"You and Droopy—see the resemblance? No? Drawn from
memory, I guess. Doubt he had his pad with him on the stairs."

"Are we supposed to know what you're talking about?"

"One of you does, at least. I'm trying to decide if it's both."

"Both what?"

"If both of you burned a man to death tonight, or if it was only
you, Seth."

"What's he talking about?" Droopy asked.

"How the hell should I know?" Seth shrieked, stripping threads
on his control.

"Because you killed him," I said.

"Killed who? What're you babbling on and on about *killing*?
Who's dead? I have no idea what you're even talking about."

"A homeless guy named Jimmy, friend of Gloria's. The one
who saw you and Droopy leaving Ted's after you killed him. He
drew that sketch."

"That's not proof of anything!" Seth tried to laugh, tried . . . just
not in him. "That doesn't even look like me. It—it could be anyone."

"Sure, but the point is, Jimmy knew it was you. Knew and didn't
say a word to anybody! He didn't give a shit you iced Ted. All he
cared about was Gloria; he wouldn't even have *thought* about
telling the cops—if you hadn't set Stosh on her. Big mistake."

It was going over Droopy's head, so I brought it down to his
level of involvement.

"How come you gave her such a hard time, anyway? What'd
Glo do to you?"

"That was all Teddy's idea," Droopy said gloomily.

"I'm talking about *after* Ted was gone. Why did you give her
up to Stosh?"

"Seth said if we kept them after her, she'd get scared and run away. If she booked outta town, then Ellis and Stosh and everyone would *know* she really took it."

"I see. . . ." And thought I really did. "But don't you mean, they'd *think* that—and not *know* you were actually responsible. Because, well, if they ever found that out, it would be the end of everything, wouldn't it? Isn't that how you saw it, Seth? You really freaked over his deal with Ted—I bet! He had no fucking idea how he'd ruined it all, did he? The access, the parties, the connections. An inside New York track money can't buy, cuz it's *invite only*, you gotta be chosen. Pissed away for a shoeful of drugs. How'd it make you feel?"

Seth held his thumbs in fists again, so much pressure I thought he'd burst them like plums. His hands shaking, tremors rode his arms. He was looking at Droopy.

"Stupid!" he spat. "Why'd you let him talk you into that? You're such a—"

Droopy reared up. "Wait a sec, you're the one who said we hadta kill him, man. Everything woulda been okay. He never woulda told Ellis. That was all just bullshit to scare us."

"Shut up!"

"Don't tell me to shut up. It's the fucking truth, you psycho."

I jumped back in not to referee but to provide chorus. "So Droopy sabotages the works, not only for him but more importantly—for *you*. You'd hitched up to his star, not knowing it was on blocks, a nobody who would drag you down to nothing. Once he was out, so were you. You had to clean up his mess. You tried to fix things by killing Ted, but they didn't stay fixed. You had Gloria still to fret over. Then today, you got a call from Jimmy, and everything fell apart. Again."

"You were there when he called," Seth accused.

"No, but I can imagine what he said. Probably threatened you unless you took the heat off Gloria. That's the kind of fair shake he'd give anyone before going to the cops. That and time enough to make up their minds."

Seth said, "I told him I couldn't make them stop. I told him they wouldn't listen to me. I told him. He said find a way."

"And so you found one. You went over and killed him."

"I didn't."

"Someone saw you in the neighborhood."

"I only went to talk to him," Seth said in a hurry. "All we did was talk."

I reached into another pocket and took out the chunky padlock, let it fall hard and heavy on the tabletop before him.

"Whoever killed Jimmy locked him in after setting the place on fire. I found this where you left it. The fire didn't touch the door, it's all in one piece, and you signed your name to it, Seth."

With my right hand, I picked up the padlock. The shackle was open and twisted over to one side. I gripped it so it stuck out like a meat hook.

"It takes hand-eye coordination to hook a vertical eyeloop. You've got to swipe at it sidewise, like this." I hooked the air, right to left. "*If* you favor your *right* hand. But a lefty comes at it this way." I switched hands and hooked an imaginary hole. "To lock it, you turn the body in to the right and push up. And when you *unlock*, it drops down and swings out, to the *left*. The way this lock was on Jimmy's door. Locked there by you."

Droopy said, "Seth . . . did you really . . ."

"That proves nothing," Seth said. "That's not proof. Are you kidding?"

"It isn't proof, you're right. It's evidence, and these days that doesn't count for much anyway. But if you want proof, I'll prove how serious I am."

I reached into a pocket and took out the hunting knife wrapped in rag. I held it over the table and unraveled the cloth. The

black-and-blue blade clattered out. The knife rolled over, and
stopped, rocking gently until still. The serrated tip pointed at Droopy.

I said to Seth, "That knife belonged to the man you killed, was
inside the shack near where they found him. See the handle
melted down? How dark the blade is?"

"So?"

"So you lit an oven and locked a man inside it! You cooked a
human being like hamburger! For that, you've got to pay. No
comps."

"You'll never prove any of it," he said. "He was a junkie squatting in a pile of sticks. Nobody cares what happened to him, nobody's ever going to believe you."

"Tell me something I don't know. You're right again, I can't
make you good for Jimmy's murder, so I won't even try. Instead
I'm going to nail you for Ted's."

Droopy broke in, "But—but—but you said you didn't care
about—"

"I still don't, but I'm calling the medical examiner's office this
morning, and telling them to take a closer look at that so-called
suicide. They'll see the screw-up, two seconds flat, and in less
time be busting the balls of the cops who signed off on it. A real
investigation will start. They'll go over Ted's place thoroughly this
time, collect every fingerprint, fiber, and scalp flake. They'll get
mountains of that *proof* you were asking about. All they'll need is
someone to match to."

I let it sink in, let them sink into it.

Seth stared down at the table, as if I hadn't spoken a word. I
couldn't tell what he was looking at: the candle, the soggy sketch,
or the burnt-handled knife. Maybe no thing.

Hoarsely, Droopy said, strangling on the enormity, "That's
not fair. It's not *my* fault, I didn't have anything to do with this
other guy's . . . I mean, come onnnnn."

"Well, you know," I said, "if you play it right with the cops,

Droopy, you might walk away. I don't see why you should be dragged down by someone else's mistake. You got cards to play. Just tie this in with the drug traffic at the Hellhole, and I think you'll find you got lots of friends over at DEA helping you to get charges reduced."

"Do you think that'll work?"

"Yeah, as long as you give up Seth first, make their job easier, they'll listen to whatever you say. Trust me."

Droopy wanted to trust, probably how he got into trouble in the first place.

I was watching Seth out of the corner of my eye. His hands flat on the table, the left one forward, daisy tattoo catching candle-glimmer. His eyes squinted at Droopy.

I said, "If you really want to cinch it, we could go down and tell them now. You'd be their fucking hero; the cops would get to bust the M.E.'s balls for a change."

Seth intruded, a sad, faraway voice, "Stop listening to him. Please."

Droopy said, "But, do you . . . do you think I should, like, get a lawyer? To, you know, negotiate, the deal?"

I shook my head gravely: no, no, no. "That's the last thing you want to do. Lawyer-up, and they'll only hit you harder. I tell you, do it my way and, who knows, you may even profit from the movie rights."

"Movie? Rights?"

Seth groaned, "Can't you *see* what he's doing? He's—"

Droopy pretended not to hear him, not to see him, not to feel the table wobbling under his stress. I ignored him, too, as if he were no longer there, only Droopy and I.

"You bet your ass, movie rights," I said. "This is the thing that sells nowadays. Kids on the streets, dance clubs and drugs. Are you shitting me? Hollywood's going to jump. And long as you aren't the one convicted, you legally stand to profit."

No idea what I was talking about, but it didn't matter, Droopy was hungry to believe. He ate it up without tasting, without chewing, swallowing huge chunks.

Seth shook the table. "What about me?" Tears crept down his cheeks, glistening worm trails. "I made a mistake. Just a mistake. A ma—"

Droopy screeched back his chair and started to rise, saying to me, "Let's split."

He never got to his feet.

Seth's left hand darted up, and a blue-black flash kicked the candle, sent it smashing to the floor, the flame in a final flare-up, then out. In the darkness, an animal's movement and cry.

I pushed off with my feet and sent my chair toppling backward. My skull hit the floor and set off a blasting cap in my brain.

Screaming and screaming, somebody was screaming.

The bartender switched on the lights, flooding the place in a harsh glare, exposing it for what it was, merely an unfinished cellar full of crappy furniture.

And two men resplendent in hot running blood. One, still seated, gushing slick ruby rivulets from his neck, the other standing over him, receiving brilliant spurts on his sopping pant leg and dripping arms, and on the wet black blade still clutched in his left hand. He was the one screaming.

Droopy sat stoically silent in shock. Real shock, of his life rudely unseated by death. The Sacred Heart tattoo cleaved open on his neck, flowing in blood blossom. Gradually, he shut off like a light on a dimmer switch.

Seth stopped his screaming. The knife fell to the floor forgotten.

By then I had scrambled crablike halfway across the room and gotten to my feet, reaching for the rail of the spiral staircase, and crawling up it two steps at a time, like some creature forced into evolution.

I met the doorman thundering down. He blocked my way, the one way out.

"What the hell's going on?" he demanded.

"Call 911. A man needs an ambulance."

The urgency in my voice was a contagion, the man's rough features went childlike and doughy. He turned and obeyed, running back toward the pay phone near the front door. I followed and kept going, straight through until outside again.

Standing in morning, total morning, God knows what time.

The city was lazy and beautiful.

I had to get home and walk the dog.

About the Author

A native of Westfield, Massachusetts, RUSSELL ATWOOD attended the American University of Washington D.C., where he co-founded the student magazine *American Library*. Afterward, he moved to New York City and served as the managing editor of *Ellery Queen's Mystery Magazine*. He has worked as an off-Broadway house manager at the Orpheum and Westside Theatres, and also as an editor at *A&E Monthly* magazine, writing the "Mystery Page" column and interviewing crime-fiction luminaries. In 1996 he published his first mystery short story (the introduction of private investigator Payton Sherwood) in *Ellery Queen*: "East of A." The namesake of that story now initiates Russell Atwood's career as a novelist. The author lives in the East Village of New York City.